# THE PHOENIX EFFECT

## PART I : THE REUNITING

# THE PHOENIX EFFECT

## PART I : THE REUNITING

# MARGARET M. MACDONALD

DRAGONBRAE

DRAGONBRAE

An Imprint of Roan & Weatherford Publishing Associates, LLC
Bentonville, Arkansas
www.roanweatherford.com

**Library of Congress Cataloging-in-Publication Data**
Names: MacDonald, Margaret M., author.
Title: The Phoenix Effect Part 1: The Reuniting | The Phoenix Effect #1
Description: First Edition. | Bentonville: Dragonbrae, 2023.
Identifiers: LCCN: 2023946495 ISBN: 978-1-63373-856-0 (hardcover) |
ISBN: 978-1-63373-857-7 (trade paperback) | ISBN: 978-1-63373-858-4 (eBook)
Subjects: | BISAC: FICTION/Science Fiction/Genetic Engineering |
FICTION/Science Fiction/Military | FICTION/Thrillers/Technological
LC record available at: https://lccn.loc.gov/2023946495

Dragonbrae trade paperback edition April, 2024

Cover & Interior Design by Casey W. Cowan
Editing by George "Clay" Mitchell & Amy Cowan

*To Mom and Dad,*
*for being brave enough to support a child in the arts*

# COLLIDING

# ONE

**ARIN'S FEET POUNDED** the street so hard his soles sent aftershocks up every bone to his skull. What had he even said? He honestly couldn't remember. Some slanderous words about the oafish Donovan, a boy—if you could even call him that—about four times Arin's size, had slithered out under his breath. He barely registered that his tongue had moved before Donovan's meaty fist made contact with the side of his head. His ear was still overheating from its impact, despite the speed enhanced wind whooshing past, drying his sun-soaked sweat as quickly as his pores produced it. Outrunning him was the only chance Arin had at avoiding any more pain, not to mention the long-lasting humiliation brought on by his slow healing bruises. The galumphing footsteps of a bearlike creature sounded out over his shoulder. He picked up speed.

Arin spotted his potential hideout, a tangle of branches overflowing the high fence around the mayor's stately mansion, as soon as he sped around the corner. Unfortunately, Donovan must have spotted Arin disappearing into them as soon as he pounded around the corner. Arin had barely tucked his foot into the brambles when he felt Donovan's vice-like grip snatch his ankle. His belly scraped the ground, his flailing arms caught the sharp points of every branch he made a desperate attempt at grabbing, as Donovan dragged him out into the open.

The next thing Arin experienced was the hard smack of iron against the back of his head. He didn't even realize he'd been hauled up to his feet. The clang of his skull hitting the fence and the subsequent ringing in his ears drowned out Donovan's words. No doubt they were some basic insult about his small, skinny physique. However much Arin loathed being called "Tiny Tim," it was at least accurate when compared to Donovan. Through watery eyes, Arin watched the meaty fist that had begun this parade of pain raise up and hover at the ready. He was about to feel its impact.

**THE VIZO WAS** droning away as usual. Lia's father had given up on attempting to shelter her from the events of the wider world. She had only ever been shooed out of the room during broadcasts about the massacre of Willowdowns, a name she had since heard repeated daily from a never-ending trail of mumbling experts. The heated protests, shouted debates, and impending sense of doom, which was once rife on the vizo, had degraded into nothing but discussion, discussion, and more discussion of the same. Lia's desire to pay attention to any of it had waned just as quickly.

Nonetheless, something about the creepy, wide-eyed Doctor Lau, a face she had seen many times before, stole her attention away from the little, metal knight and dragon she had been imaging into a fierce battle for dominance. Papa was equally transfixed and punctuated the end of each sentence the good doctor stuttered out with a disapproving "Hrmph."

On the shimmering vizo, Doctor Lau knotted his fingers as he spoke. *"We continue to work every day. There will be a way to improve the formula, to fill in the gaps."*

The knotting went on as the calm-voiced interviewer melodically countered, *"Yet there have been no subsequent improvements since the first generation of the formula. Should we really continue to use a technology that robs us of love, desire, excitement, joy, every emotion that makes us human?"*

Doctor Lau's retort was quick. *"Injections are voluntary."*

Papa scoffed at the screen.

*"Not in the Unified Army,"* the interviewer was equally quick to point out. Papa raised his glass to that.

*"We are obligated to protect those who protect us."* Doctor Lau was staring into some great distance beyond the interviewer. It made Lia wonder what he could possibly be looking at.

*"You claim we are far from the days of the Willowdowns,"* the interviewer went on, *"but how can we prevent such tragedies when a virtually immortal and completely emotionless army increases its numbers daily?"*

The doctor's eyes somehow found an even greater distance to fixate upon. He sat, completely frozen, except for the slightest visible tensing in his jaw. After a long pause, his eyes flicked back toward the interviewer. A single syllable was the last sound Doctor Lau got out before Lia's father shut off the vizo, returning his view of the pastoral painting he kept behind the clear screen to restore his calm after watching the news. He concluded this viewing session with his own statement. "Not in my town."

As he took himself back to the bar to refresh his drink, Lia rolled toward the window so he wouldn't notice she had been watching the vizo too. She made a show of playing her game, using the spot of sunshine on the carpet as her stage. She crashed the knight's sword into the dragon, let out her own version of a dying dragon's agonizing cry, and dropped it to the ground. She propped the knight up on the windowsill and was musing over his tiny, proud silhouette, when a flash of movement outside caught her eye. That scrawny figure that had just been yanked out of the bushes looked familiar.

**ARIN'S EYES WERE** still watering when Donovan suddenly released him and went reeling backwards. Where was it, the bone crunching sound, the sudden onslaught of blinding pain? Arin had no idea how he'd come to be standing against the fence with not so much as one of Donovan's fingers on him… until he looked up.

Lia was straddling the branch of a gnarled, old tree over Arin's head, pelting rocks at Donovan. Arin glanced back and forth as Donovan attempted to return fire, miserably missing with every shot. Lia gripped her last weapon and launched from the shoulder. The rock pinged Donovan between the eyes. He palmed his forehead in shock, then stared in even greater shock at the blot of blood staining his hand.

"You're gonna pay for this!" was the only thing he blurted out before running away. Arin couldn't be sure, but he'd swear he saw Donovan's shoulders surge from an uncontrollable sob.

Lia launched herself out of the tree like an acrobat and landed with a thud behind Arin. He turned and stared at her through the bars of the fence, unsure of what was supposed to happen next. Fighting was something he'd seen her do plenty of times before, usually when someone dared to imply that the mayor's precious daughter was too delicate for roughhousing on the playground. She's never done it on his behalf before. Come to think of it, they'd never even spoken to each other before. Arin figured he'd better start with "Um… thanks."

Lia returned his thanks with a hard, analytical stare. Was she about to tell him that he probably deserved it? Was that why she'd never bothered with him before, just another of his classmates who detested his high marks and otherwise thought he was a waste of space? He couldn't tell what she was thinking, but something about her eyes held his glued in place. She had just opened her mouth to speak when one of the grand doors of the mansion creaked open. The mayor's voice barked out. "Lianna! Get back in here!"

His booming bark made Arin jump, but Lia didn't even flinch. She kept her eyes fixed on Arin and said, "You owe me." Then she turned and scampered over to her father.

Arin watched the hulking Mayor McMillan usher Lia inside, muttering something about her ruining another dress. The door sealed them in with a dull boom. Arin simply stood and stared. The ceaseless thudding in his head, the burning pain of every scratch, the swamp of sweat gathering at the small of his back should have outweighed all other physical sensations, but something else had swept in to overtake the discomfort. A tingle of excitement rose up from his chest and threw warmth into his cheeks. Even through all his pain, Arin could feel himself smiling.

**THE IRONY OF** having rocks pelted at him on a regular basis was lost on Arin. Seventeen years had passed since he had been saved by them, seven of those spent under the influence of the world's greatest medical achievement and in service of the world's most formidable army. Now, oppressing regular protests from the quarry was simply one of his daily responsibilities. Taking the occasional hit from a freshly carved chunk of stone was all in the line of duty.

Corwin was taking the tight turns through the narrow stone corridors of Caldera City at a neck-breaking speed. He had come to know the route from the barracks to the quarry well enough by now. Arin just hoped that the tell-tale whine of the engine was loud enough to keep people out of the transport's path. Most of the streets were still deep in shadow. Early morning sun cast slashes of light across their path and made the dusty air look like walls attempting to keep them at bay. They broke through another and another. The gate between the city walls and the quarry lay just ahead. It was open barely as wide as the transport itself, as if the Masons were daring the Guard to come through at full speed. Corwin would take that dare without a second thought. The threat of a crash was hardly a deterrent for the Unity Guard. He sped through the opening, into the full sun of the quarry, and slammed the transport to a halt, rising a tidal wave of dust.

The first crash of mineral on metal was muted inside the armored vehicle, but as the doors slid open and the contingent of guards poured out, the chaotic din of shouting poured in. It soon mingled with the loud cracks of stone hitting bone. The tidily uniformed bodies raced into the pit of dust covered Masons. The Guards spread out quickly, like black ants overtaking an enemy colony. Each blow only stalled them for the seconds it took their bloody gashes to heal. They shook off each shattering impact as if it were nothing more than falling rain.

The Mason's became one writhing huddle in the middle of the quarry as the Guard surrounded, guns at the ready.

*Bang!* Arin's shot into the air brought silence and stillness. He hadn't bothered to join the crowd. What good was beating one man at a time when he could silence the whole mess at once? That was, after all, the instinct that had brought him a command post. Strategy over strength was not a popular view among Unity soldiers, but his orders didn't have to be popular to be obeyed. Arin stood on top of the vehicle, assuring his lean form looked replete with authority to all those below, including his own Guard.

"Stand down, soldiers!" he shouted. A momentary air of hesitance rippled throughout the crowd before the Guards holstered their guns and backed away from the huddled handful of Masons. *"Fall in!"*

The Guards raced to form a neat line in front of the vehicle. All but Corwin, who first faked a quick step toward the huddle of Masons, just to make them flinch. He took full advantage of his authority as Arin's second to use strength over strategy as often as possible. One would think he got pleasure out of watching the uninjected leap back in fear, if it were possible for him to feel any pleasure.

"This is a Unified city now." Arin addressed the Masons below. "Under full Unity authority. You will live as Unified citizens, and you will work as Unified citizens."

"We can't keep these hours, these quotas." a gristled man yelled out from the crowd.

"We're not like you. We're too weak!" another dusty sounding voice added.

Arin was in the midst of a diplomatic pause when Corwin interjected. "You're strong enough to throw those rocks."

The gristled man, safe in the center of the huddle, didn't hesitate to retort. "Why don't you people work the quarry if it's so precious to your damn Unity!"

Corwin charged out of line. The huddle bent away as he approached.

"Corwin!" He froze at the sound of Arin's voice but did not turn around. "Use your strength only where it is necessary, Sub-Commander." Corwin kept his eyes fixed on the gristled man as he backed away and returned to his place in line. He'd never stepped out of the line-up before they were assigned to Caldera, but the number of times Arin had had to order him back had only increased since their arrival. It was as if the dust and sun were grinding away the patience Corwin's nanites should have granted him. Fortunately, Arin still had his, even though this less than prestigious post on the backwards fringe had done its fair share of grinding at him.

Arin turned his attention back to the Masons. "You work the hours. You fill the quotas. You follow Unity law, and you don't question it. Those of you who choose to do otherwise are free to head for the open desert." He gestured toward the undulating hills of sunbaked emptiness just beyond the quarry and scanned the crowd, assessing. He had instilled enough fear to silence them but would drop one more grain of it before leaving. "Be warned, this is the last time I will call back my Guard."

"I'll believe that when I see it." Corwin muttered under his breath. Arin's hearing was exceptional. It had already been perfect before the enhancement of his nanites had increased it to a near animal-like sensitivity. Fortunately, the nanites had also suppressed his tendency to lash out when provoked. His inner strategist had taken over.

"And to assure you meet those quotas, I'll be leaving Guards on watch. Assign accordingly, Sub-Commander." There, Arin thought, he had scratched Corwin's itch and handed him the authority he craved in the same breath. Maybe that would save him a bit of lip for the rest of the day. Arin jumped down and took his seat inside the transport as Corwin ordered his soldiers of choice—the largest of course—to their various posts around the quarry. The remainder of the Guard filed in. Corwin jumped into the driver's seat and pulled the vehicle away from the quarry with a determined speed. The morning sun flashed white across the window, then disappeared behind the towering buildings as they sped back into the narrow streets of Caldera.

There was only a moment's silence before Corwin spoke. "We need to suppress these outbreaks before the head counsel's arrival."

It would seem his itch was not yet gone. Arin needed to remind him who was in charge. "Was that an order, Sub-Commander?"

"Only a suggestion, sir." That was about as polite as he ever was. "He's not going to be concerned with a handful of workers pitching rocks. These people are no threat to us."

"It's not the image we want to present, Commander." It was a valid point. Arin had to give it due consideration, though he didn't have to agree right away. He fixed his eyes on the road ahead and took the time to consider in silence.

They turned down a narrow lane-way. The silhouettes of two small children playing a ballgame occupied the other end of the lane. Fortunately, Corwin had reduced to a civilian friendly speed. A woman hurried out in a flurry of fabric, grabbed their hands, and pulled both children inside, as if the still distant vehicle were on the verge of crushing them both. Arin kept his eyes fixed on the humble home that they disappeared into as the transport glided past. Frightened eyes peered out through cracks between wooden shutters. What were they so afraid of? Arin mused over the question, letting it sink in deep. For a moment, he felt his own brow furrowed in concern. Then, as if a switch flipped inside him, the physical sensation and the question that had stirred it both evaporated. He snapped back into placid calm.

Arin cleared his throat before speaking, not because he needed to, but to assure he was heard. "Have the central corridor cleared out before sunset."

"Yes, sir."

He knew Corwin would jump on that duty as soon as they returned to headquarters and give him a few hours of peace in the process. Arin returned to scanning the streets as they glided back to the barracks, not because he expected to encounter any trouble, but because it maintained his air of authority. Strategy over strength. Unfortunately, his keen eyes and sharp hearing had just missed the hooded stranger slinking through the shadows behind them.

**LIA WAS GRATEFUL** she managed to get to Caldera City when she did. It had taken three days alone to make a mental map of the maze of twisted streets, cloistered from the sun by a jumbled mass of stone and mud-brick towers. The Unity flag was already flying from every turret when she arrived. Had the intel come to them any later, she would have missed the head counsel's arrival altogether. He'd be safely locked in the barracks and yet another border city would belong to the Unity. It was bound to happen anyway, but at least she had the chance to make it a bit harder for them, to undercut the egos of the poker-faced authorities and their robotic masses.

Right, left, down the hill, at the end of the lane-way, sat the shady little day-night eatery and tavern, her destination and headquarters for the moment. It was only a matter of hours now, and she preferred to wait among the chatter of locals. The bartender was still taking upend-ed chairs off the tables when Lia's shadow crossed into the rectangle of light pouring through the door. She pulled back her hood, and he squinted to focus on her face. "You're not one of my usual early risers." he said with a smile, inviting an introduction.

"I was just after some breakfast." Subtly avoiding any direct con-versation about who she was or where she came from had become second nature to her.

"I'll fire up the processor." The bartender hopped behind the bar and flipped a switch on a large metal box with a chute aimed down toward a pile of plates. The air filled with the white noise of mechan-ical vibration.

"A double golden wouldn't hurt either." Lia added. The bartender raised his eyebrows. She knew that would spark a bit too much inter-est, but nerves were getting the better of her. "I got a long day ahead of me," she casually explained. The bartender nodded and served her a healthy dose of golden-brown liquor from an unlabeled bottle. Must be the desert's finest, she thought, as a smile crossed her face.

A broad, hairy ape of a man marched in, accompanied by a curvaceous and scantily clad woman, who left no room for doubt about her profession. He stumbled into the chairs, making the woman cackle like a hen.

"You've got to be kidding me, Johnson. You've got build duty in less than an hour!" the bartender shouted at him.

He waved off his concern with a large, sail-like hand. "Rita and I was just out enjoying the night is all. Only, all of a sudden, night turned to morning. Sneaky that!" He laughed a full hardy laugh and pounded the same large hand on the bar. Tiny waves crisscrossed in Lia's glass from its impact.

"He just needs some food. He'll be fine." Rita interjected. "Won't you, hon?"

"Right-o!" Johnson declared.

The bartender acquiesced and threw a few brown blocks into the vibrating processor. A slimy brown sludge was beginning to ooze out of the shoot and fill up the first plate. The prospect of that as her breakfast threatened to turn Lia's stomach. She decided to settle it by throwing back the rest of her drink in one go.

Johnson and Rita scrapped their way onto the bar stools one over from Lia. Johnson focused his wobbly vision on the tiny vizo box across the bar. The picture jumped and fuzzed too much to be worth watching, but the bold, pointed symbol of the Unity remained steadfast in the corner of the screen.

"What have you got that shatz on the vizo for?" Johnson asked as he pointed a sausage finger in its direction.

The bartender rolled his eyes. He was already tired of this argument. "Don't start in on that again. I don't follow the new regulations, I get shut down, then where are you going to drag your sorry arse to sober up before work?"

"Grow a set, man! They can't tell us what to watch."

"Yes, they can." Lia interjected. Rita and Johnson stared at her as if she had just appeared out of thin air. "But it won't matter if you follow regulations. Refuse injection, and they'll run you out of business anyway." Lia knew she shouldn't have said anything, but she almost couldn't help it. Their ignorance would eventually be crushed by the truth. At least it was better to get a little warning first.

"No way," the bartender countered. "I was given a license, nice and legal-like."

"Did you check the expiration date?" Lia asked. The bartender searched his memory, doubt in his eyes.

"Bah!" Johnson's volume gave everyone a start. "You're just a dust dweller, like the rest of us. What do you know?"

"Enough to know that your arse will definitely get arrested for showing up at your post like that or worse. I recommend having a little coffee with your breakfast."

Johnson scrapped his way up and half-kicked, half-bumped into the bar stool, which subsequently slapped to the floor. Lia jumped to her feet and reached for the hidden gun at her back but stopped just short of pulling it. A big man with a delicate ego was not the emergency situation she carried it for. Nevertheless, the feel of its grip always helped to steel her nerves.

Johnson hovered his hulking form over her. "And what gives you the right to tell me what to do?" The fumes of his long night with Rita practically oozed out his skin. Lia briefly considered pulling her gun just to get him to back off so she could breathe. "I don't see any stars on your chest." His sausage finger was a hair away from poking her in the sternum, and most likely being snapped off for doing so, when an authoritative voice froze him on the spot.

"I got three right here." A stout silhouette in the proud cut of a Unity uniform filled the doorway. Lia immediately released the hold on her gun and cast her eyes down. The Unity soldier, an Elite Guard sub-commander by the color of his stripes and aforementioned number of stars, strode in and put himself between Lia and Johnson. "Are you a problem for this woman?" he asked Johnson with one hand resting comfortably on his holster. He must have read Lia's posture as that of a demure little desert flower who needed saving, rather than a woman who simply couldn't chance being recognized.

"No, sir." Johnson said with a slack jaw.

The sub-commander gave the other slack-jawed onlookers and the eatery itself a disinterested once over. He glanced over his shoulder at Lia but didn't hover long enough for her to have to force out the thanks he undoubtedly thought he had earned. He turned to the bartender. "This establishment is to be cleared out and closed by seventeen hundred hours today." The bartender stammered. "Are we understood, barkeep?"

"All due respect, sir, night is my busiest time."

"Not tonight." He directed the next words at Johnson again. "Are we going to have a problem?"

"No! I'll close up. Seventeen hundred. Yes, sir." The bartender was more eager to have this moment pass than he was to raise any protest. The Unity sub-commander nodded, took one more passing look at Lia, and marched away. Rita turned her slack expression back toward the bar. Johnson silently picked up and returned to his bar stool, his ego sufficiently shattered to bits.

Lia released tension from her clenched-up fists. She couldn't chance leaving now, no matter how badly she wanted to escape her contentious company. The Guard would need time to finish sweeping the street clean of its own locals. At least there was one way to occupy her time. Lia pushed her empty glass toward the bartender as said, "I'll need another."

# TWO

**IT WAS NOTHING** but a ceremonial display of power. Arin knew they were key to maintaining order. Show your numbers. Show your discipline. Show your strength. Respect will follow. That had been the long-standing strategy employed by the Unity Army, and it continued to work with every new territory they gained. Nonetheless, Arin would rather have been taking rocks to the head than be another puppet in this theater of authority. He probably would have loathed every second of this contrived act if he were capable of loathing.

Every soldier was in the neatest of lines, surrounding the already impenetrable fortress of stone. Arin's Guard formed a gauntlet up either side of the staircase leading toward its steel doors. From his post at the top, he could see down into the surrounding streets. They were quiet, entirely devoid of life. He glanced up at the sentinel's post, but her silhouette had disappeared from the roof's edge. She was probably needlessly walking its perimeter, but he didn't require her merely ceremonial signal anyway. The flash of sunlight off polished metal revealed that the head counsel's vehicle had made the final turn on its approach to headquarters.

*"Attention!"* Arin barked out. His Guard followed suit, straightening up those last few vertebrae. A ripple of mimicked action followed from the soldiers surrounding the fortress. It was almost beautiful in its uniformity. The shiny transport, bearing only a hint of the surrounding dust on its underside, hummed to a stop at the bottom of the stairs. The side door slid open, and the head counsel, a man with a

fiercely lined face, emerged into the long rays of evening light. He surveyed the lines of soldiers with an inscrutable gaze. A young but equally fierce jawed woman, presumably the assistant counsel, stepped out behind him. With a nod to each other, they began to ascend the steps toward Arin. He lifted his chin and waited in stiff, ceremonial silence.

A shot ripped through the air. The head counsel dropped. A large hole in the side of his head spilled dark blood onto the dusty steps. Arin launched himself down the staircase, threw his body around the assistant counsel, and dragged her stumbling back down the steps. High caliber bullets sent spurts of dust up around him as he forced her back into the transport. Every solider armed their weapons, as if still in ceremonial unison. A moment of tense silence followed as they waited for another shot.

*Crack!* A bullet exploded the stone behind Arin's head. His eyes darted up toward the source, the sentinel's absent post on the rooftop. An armor clad assassin, silhouetted by the glow of the low sun, ducked behind the roof's edge

"That rooftop! Surround the building!" Arin commanded. Soldiers rushed, en-mass, toward the foreboding stone walls. Arin, leading the charge, was the first to leap up and begin climbing the building's rough facade. He leapt from one stone up to the next, confident in the grip of his boots and the strength of his hold. The silhouette of a hand appeared above and dropped a small object over his head. Arin pressed hard against the stone. The object whooshed past his ear and exploded on contact with the soldier below him, vibrating a cascade of sand down the facade. Through dust-clouded eyes Arin watched the entire contingent at his back tumble to the ground in a burst of fire and flailing limbs. They would recover but not quickly enough. This pursuit was his alone for now. He turned back to his climbing and picked up speed.

Arin swung up onto the roof. His sentinel was nowhere to be seen, but he didn't have time to seek her out. The assassin was already a dot in the distance, speeding toward the neighboring rooftop. Arin pulled out his gun and fired. The bullet grazed the assassin's arm in the midst of a jump from one roof to next. The deadly rifle dropped between the buildings and clattered to the street below. The assassin managed a last-minute snatch of the edge of the next building, then scrambled up and disappeared into the tangle of rusted machinery jutting out of the rooftop.

Arin jogged for the edge, leapt across the gap with grace, and landed neatly on his feet. He kept his gun at the ready and his eyes sharp as he entered the maze of machinery. He snapped, gun first, around one corner. Silence. Stillness. He rounded another, nothing but rusted ducts and ventilation pipes. He waited, listening. Arin's ears picked up the slightest crunch of a footfall, but it was too late.

The assassin snapped a choke wire over his head. Arin threw his weight back, flipped the assassin over his body, and ripped away the wire. His own blood stained his fingertips, a wheeze of air pushed out through the break in his windpipe, but the slice around his neck healed instantly.

The assassin scampered away and deftly launched into a blackened vent. Arin reached the vent in time to see the assassin sliding down into darkness. He holstered his gun and leapt in after. He braced with his palms to control his descent, grinding them to a bloody pulp against the rusted metal. Surely, he thought, the descent would be even more damaging to the assassin. Arin prepared himself to meet with a crumpled body at the bottom as he rocketed out of the vent, but all he encountered was a knee-deep layer of ash in the base of old furnace. His solid landing kicked up a thick gray cloud. He raised his gun to the assassin's misty shape beyond the cloud, but Arin hadn't seen the lump of steel in her hand.

A hard *smack* cracked into the bone of his forearm and sent Arin's gun clattering into the furnace. He snatched at the next swing and brought the makeshift weapon to a dead stop. Arin pushed forward, forcing the assassin to skid out into the room beyond, and cracked the lump of steel in half with one twist of his fist. The assassin could only take one step back before Arin had thrown her to the ground. He pinned her down and ripped off her helmet. The deadly assassin he had just pursued, the enemy he now had below him, was Lia.

Arin and Lia stared at each other, frozen by inescapable shock. For a split second, Arin saw the eight-year-old girl that was once looking at him through the iron fence. The flood of images and sensations that followed defied explanation. Moments from the entirety of their lives together flashed through his mind. With each, followed a hint of the emotions these moments had once carried with them. Tiny electric shocks of joy, frustration, lust, sadness, love, and pain all hit his body at once. Memories of Lia had come and gone over the years but, like all else Arin had experienced since his injection, they had been dull and muted, as if hopelessly lost in a fog. At this moment, he experienced these closely guarded memories, these long-suppressed sensations, physical and emotional, with the clarity of a bright summer day.

He had no idea how long he had been incapacitated by this experience. It could have been mere seconds in which he relived all those years, but the noises from a lower level told him it had been too long. Lia attempted to squirm away. Arin pinned her down and whispered "Shh! They'll hear you." She stared into his eyes, trying to read his intentions. Arin couldn't have explained them if he tried. All he could think was if they find her, they will kill her. I won't let that happen.

Another noise echoed up from downstairs, this one closer. Lia attempted to squirm away again. Arin held her firm, clasped tight to her mouth, but that threw her into a state of frantic twisting. In a moment of desperation, Arin dug his finger into the oozing bullet wound on Lia's arm. She flailed like a dying fish and emitted a muffled scream into his palm. Then her body seized, and she passed out.

Arin loosened his grip. He absorbed the sight of Lia lying before him, his placid calm completely removed. Her fate was entirely in his hands. She was either going to become an enemy captured by his quick decisive action or evidence of his betrayal. He couldn't accept her as an enemy, and the evidence needed to be hidden. He took a quick survey of the machinery in the room. A conveyor belt that would have once carried scrap into the massive furnace he had landed in had a concealed engine, just big enough for a human. He carried Lia's limp body across the room, ripped off the facing of the rusted-out engine, folded her limbs delicately into the gears, and cuffed her hands into the depths of the machinery. Action was slowly restoring his inner strategist. This would work. He was sure of it. Calm began to return. He found himself reaching toward her cheek, then, as if he feared the effect that skin on skin contact might have on him, he snapped his hand back and sealed Lia inside the engine.

"Commander Arin!" Corwin called out, his voice still muffled by a few floors.

With a single breath Arin reset into the firm strategist he had been before he saw Lia's face. He stirred the ash to cover their tracks, wiped her blood from his hands, holstered his fallen gun, and backed out of the room.

**"SLOPPY. NEGLIGENT. THIS** is *not* how I want to describe the actions of my Elite Guard commander." Arin stood at attention opposite the assistant counsel's wide desk in the cell-like room. She rhythmically tapped the desk as she demanded "Explain to me how you, the leader of your unit, the fastest in your Guard, the first to reach the rooftop, were unable to capture a lone shooter."

"The assassin had knowledge of the city's infrastructure. He knew where to run. The investigation will—"

"We shouldn't need an investigation." Arin had practiced that line many times in his head but had no idea how to retort to her interruption of it. He was not accustomed to being disciplined. He was even less accustomed to lying. She took his pause as an invitation, stepped around the desk, and came nose to nose with him. "I realize that, as a Guard commander from a central city, you probably thought watching over this sandy piece of shatz in the middle of nowhere was a joke. But this, Commander Arin, is where our war for unification is fought and won."

"The war is long over."

"Our leader is dead. There is no stronger declaration of war." Arin could not argue. The assistant counsel took another lap of her desk. "I have no choice but to subject you to a memory review."

Of all the possible scenarios Arin had run through his mind while marching back to headquarters, that was the last and most extreme. His voice softened as he asked, "And what will you do with me while you sift through my recordings?"

"You're the strategist. What would you do with a potential traitor while you scanned his nanites for evidence?"

"Keep him in the brig." As if the prospect of having fluid siphoned right of his brain, of having his past actions, public and private, scanned and analyzed by a military investigator, wasn't unappealing enough, it also came with the promise of being locked up indefinitely. Of course, that was only until they found the recordings that revealed him hiding Lia, then he'd be marched out to die. "Counsel, my record of impeccable service would indicate no need for such methods, and my investigations have always yielded beneficial results for the Unity." It was ironic that enduring loyalty was his best defense at that moment.

This time she managed to silence him with the raising of a single finger. "You have till tomorrow morning to dig up your phantom trail. If you don't turn up any evidence by then, I'll just have to pull it straight out of your head." Arin found himself wondering if he would have been any better off under the thumb of the man whose body now lay in cold storage. "You're dismissed, Commander."

Arin maintained his firm jaw and soldier's stance, but inside his mind was reeling. Every possible argument against her decision raced through his thoughts, but he knew none of them were strong enough to change her mind. He gave her a stiff a salute and opened the door.

Corwin was standing on the other side.

"Come in, Sub-Commander." the assistant counsel ordered over Arin's shoulder. They slid past each other in the doorway, the static charge of tension between them. Corwin gave Arin a small nod before closing the door behind him.

The foreboding realization that his subordinate had been asked to meet the assistant counsel without him was quickly overtaken by the urgent need to secure his fate. It had to begin with Lia. Keeping her hidden was key. Together they might even be able to produce a shred of evidence that would satisfy the Unity and throw them off her trail. But why would she help him? She was his enemy, through and through. So why had he saved her?

If it hadn't been for the deep distraction of those unanswerable questions dancing through his mind as he walked out of headquarters and into the winding streets of Caldera, Arin would have noticed he was being followed.

**THE BEAUTIFUL IMAGES** Lia once associated with youthful innocence were jumbled together with a mess of dark memories. Pastoral greenery became fiery explosions of urban rubble. Birdsong became the sound of gunfire and the screams of pain. Arin was there too. The skinny little boy looking at her through the fence morphed into the hard-edged man who stared down at her with eyes that sat somewhere between cold and confounded. There was a spark within them, hidden deep, but as her visions took her closer in, the spark became a flame and rose into a screaming inferno. Lia awoke with a start.

Her first instinct was to break free and run like a rabbit escaping a trap, but her movement was instantly halted by a clang of metal and the pull of handcuffs against her wrists. She steadied her breathing and took in her surroundings. A razor-thin shaft of light revealed the coffin-like confines of her hiding place and that it was still daylight. Unity soldiers could be near. She stilled her body, closed her eyes, and listened. Whether it was minutes or hours, the silence became too oppressive to bear, so she began to pull against the handcuffs.

Sweat was dripping down her forehead, and the skin around her wrists was raw and burning when the shaft of light finally disappeared. Now entirely blind, she began to feel her way around. She methodically mapped the gears she could reach with her one free foot and wandering fingertips. She rattled what she could with her body, sounding out which parts were loose and likely to break. She was keeping herself occupied to prevent thoughts of what could happen to her from overtaking her reasonable mind. She had just determined to do this over and over and over again, as long as it took, when her fingers unexpectedly traced across a clump of machinery degraded by rust.

With energy restored by hope, she slid the handcuffs over to the rusty spot, took in another deep breath, and pulled. Once, twice, with the third painful yank she broke free. Lia slammed her body against what she'd already determined to be the loosened shell of her machinery prison and tumbled out. She hadn't even gotten to her knees when a whoosh of air through the ash below revealed a door nearby being opened. She snatched up the piece of rusted pipe that had tumbled out with her, pushed up to her feet, and disappeared into the shadows.

Lia peered into the moonlit room from her patch of darkness. Arin entered. His gun was in one hand, a paper wrapped package was tucked under his other arm. He approached the engine that had been her prison and stooped to examine her footprints in the ash. Lia emerged from the darkness, rusty pipe in hand. She raised it over her head and took one step closer. Arin whipped around and pointed his gun straight into her face. They both froze in place.

He was the first to break their lengthy silence. "I'm not here to hurt you."

There was no way to know if he meant that, no intonation in his voice, no spark in his eyes. Had she only imagined that she'd seen one? Only his actions would tell her one way or the other. "Then put away the gun."

"Drop your weapon, and I'll consider it."

Lia dropped the pipe, knowing it was useless anyway. Arin lowered his gun, just enough to look her in the eye, but kept it firmly aimed in her direction. His spark-less eyes traced over her body armor. Lia kept her gaze straight ahead and face inscrutable as he examined her.

Eventually he asked, "Are you alone?"

"Is this a formal interrogation?" Refusing any straight answers was her default.

"It's been years, Lia. For all I knew, you could have been dead." Even those words, the sound of her own name coming out of his mouth, had nothing but emptiness behind them. It made her angry.

"And I thought *you* were. Frankly, I'd made my peace with it." Lia said as coldly as her fear allowed.

"I'm not going to let you disappear on me."

"So, arrest me, then. Isn't that what you tin cans do to Resistors?" It didn't matter to her that it was Arin inside that uniform. He was one of them.

"Far worse. But as I said, that's not what I'm here for." She couldn't help but step back as he approached. Her eyes flicked down to the hand that was reaching into his pocket, but what he pulled out was the keys to the handcuffs. She remained dead still as he unlocked the handcuffs, her eyes fixed on his gun. He dropped the package at her feet and instructed. "Put that on."

She bent down, keeping her eyes planted on Arin's gun as she opened the package. She pulled out a skimpy dress and immediately knew where he'd procured it. She tossed it to the ground with disdain. "I'm not going to be a part of some twisted, poker face fantasy."

"Would you rather chance being recognized? You won't pass for Unity, and none of these dust dwellers walk around in body armor."

"Are you going to imprison me in the city brothel?"

"Get dressed." She stood defiant. Protesting everything he asked for felt as if it was giving her strength or at least helping to tamp down her fear. He raised his gun again and demanded, "Now."

Lia pulled off her armor piece by piece, taking her time. She gave him another stubborn pause before stripping off her clothes. As the layers peeled away, the collection of scars across her torso was revealed. They were a part of her body she always chose to conceal because of the many questions they arose and the memories that came with them. They were also the one part of her body Arin had never seen since they'd only entered her world after Arin had chosen to leave it. Lia's gaze was still fixed on his gun, but she could feel Arin's eyes scanning over her scars.

"Has it been that long since you've seen a woman undress?" She took his wandering eyes as another opportunity to undermine him. It was the only defense she had left. "I should think not, or where would you have gotten the dress?"

She glanced up at his face and caught a wrinkle on his brow. The spark in his eyes was there too, but it looked different now. It wasn't confusion. It was concern. The sight of her scars had disturbed him. How was that possible? She quickly pulled the dress over her body, concealing the vicious scars once again. Arin's attention snapped back to Lia's face, and the furrow of concern disappeared instantly.

"Put your hands up," he instructed.

Her eyes followed his hands again as he holstered his gun, reached into another of what seemed like countless pockets, and pulled out a medic-kit. A scan of his uniform as he crossed the patch of moonlight between them told her he was four-star Elite Guard commander. It instilled her with a renewed touch of fear as he approached, but all he did was gently grasp her wrist and lower her injured arm.

Arin began to clean Lia's bullet wound. She attempted to keep a side eye on his gun but was overtaken by a sharp sting of pain in her arm. She winced despite her best efforts to retain a stony demeanor. He paused and looked into her face as if analyzing her pain levels, then finished cleaning with a gentler touch and smoothed a bandage over her wound. The task was complete, but he kept a hold on her wrist. They locked eyes in silence.

"*Freeze!*" a deep voice shouted from the corner. The stout sub-commander from the eatery emerged from the shadows, his gun aimed toward them.

Arin whirled in his direction. Lia's opportunity had finally come. She whipped Arin's gun out of his holster and took aim at the sub-commander.

Arin stepped between them and commanded "Stand down. *Now!*"

He looked at the bandage on Lia's arm, the pile of body armor at her feet, then back up Arin. The next words almost slithered out of his mouth. "I'm not taking orders from a traitor."

**CORWIN AND LIA** both sidestepped Arin. Lia got in the first shot, straight to Corwin's chest. He was already dropping when he fired. His shot ricochet around the room, blasting the air with metallic pings. Arin dove at Lia, taking her to the ground, but before he could get a grip on his gun, she had it aimed firmly at his temple.

"I know exactly where to put a hole that won't heal," she declared. He tried to see past her hard stare. She wouldn't. She couldn't, not to him. But she had already killed. What would stop her now? These thoughts ripped through Arin's mind in an instant. Despite any doubt in what she might be capable of, he had no choice but to release her.

As Lia squirmed away, another gunshot blasted over their heads. Arin's eyes snapped back to Corwin. The bullet fell from his chest as he sat up and took aim at Lia. She darted away from the next series of shots, raced for the window, smashed through the glass, and disappeared down the fire escape. Corwin turned his aim on Arin.

Arin had already weighed up his options while Corwin's stray shots were cracking around the room. Even with the nanites swimming through his blood, Corwin was a creature of impulse. Strength over strategy. Even if Arin could conjure up some explanation for what he had just seen, Corwin would fill him with bullets before he let him speak one word of it. Arin could either let himself be disabled or be the disabler.

Arin flew at Corwin and rammed him to the ground. He snatched Corwin's wrist and smacked his gun hand into a pile of rusted metal, spiking him through the palm. Arin reached for his fallen gun. Corwin ripped his hand free and shoved him back by the throat. Arin swung with all his might, smashing into Corwin's nose. He pulled back only long enough to release another blow, then another and another. Arin pummeled Corwin until his face was a bloody mess. Arin only stopped when he heard the wheeze of a word bubble out Corwin's mouth. "I," he choked out through the blood, "am Commander now."

The time for conjuring up lies and falsifying evidence had passed. Corwin would never let go of the command he had obviously been promised for uncovering Arin's secret. Arin had no recourse left, no other strategy to turn to. He jumped up, ran across room, and dove out the window.

# THREE

**THE POUNDING OF** Arin's boots echoed around the narrow streets. Corwin wouldn't have even waited for his wounds to heal before calling Arin's own Guard on him. There was no point in attempting to quietly sneak away, to disappear. His only chance now was to outrun them. Ahead of him, Lia's lithe silhouette dashed around a corner. At least he knew what he was running toward. As Arin sped around the corner, he spotted Lia's hands disappearing down a shaft into the water pipes below the city. The echoes of his bootfalls were joined by others racing down the distant streets at his back. He doubled his speed, dove to the ground, and slid into the shaft.

Arin splashed into ankle-deep water. He stilled, let his eyes adjust to the darkness, and listened. Sloshing sounded out from another tunnel. Arin followed the sounds around one turn, another. The pipes became more and more narrow, forcing him into a crouch as he raced deeper into the darkness. He reached an intersection of pipes and came to a standstill. He listened again, but everything around him had gone quiet. Only the gentle *drip, drip, drip* of condensation filled the silence.

"Why did you follow me?" Lia's low voice bounced around the empty tunnel.

Arin spun around, trying to spot her in the darkness. "I didn't have a choice."

"You could have chosen not to lock me in a box, like a trapped animal waiting to be slaughtered." Her accusatory words ghosted all around him. She was close.

"I could have chosen to arrest you. To watch you face death for your crime." Arin peered into every adjoining tunnel as he spoke, looking for any trace of her. "But I didn't. I chose to do whatever I could to save your life."

"Now you've put both our lives at risk."

"I was dead, anyway. They want to extract my recordings. They would see the moment I hid you. They would know that I helped a dangerous Resistor." He waited for a response, another hint of her location, but only encountered more *drip, drip, dripping.* "You know what that means. They would see you, see your face. You might have had a chance at hiding, but not when every soldier in the Unity can identify you." He waited through a moment of silence but somehow knew she hadn't left. He was starting to get through to her. A distant splash from another tunnel made it clear he had little time left. He closed his eyes, whispered, "Please, Lia," then stood in silence and awaited her verdict.

A hand dropped onto his shoulder. Lia was reaching down from a tight crawl space above him. "Climb up. Follow me."

Arin instinctively kept count of each turn they made as he slid behind her through the crawl space. She pushed along with her uninjured arm and one leg that was freed up by an intentional tear through the dress. It must have been slowing her down. She stopped, twisted her body around, and dropped, feet first, through an open vent. Arin followed, preparing himself to be confronted by anything as he dropped into the unknown.

He landed in a round chamber surrounded by hatches sealed against the water. There was a travel pack in the center and a single lamp bathing the metal room in yellow light. Lia dug into the travel pack, pulled out a chunky gun with a long barrel, and turned it on Arin.

"I thought you were going to help." Arin said as he put his hands up and backed away.

She followed, keeping aim at his chest. "This is help. Those soldiers are tracking your biosignal as we speak. The tunnels will dampen it for a while, but we won't last the night if they find you."

Arin shouted *"Wait!"* but heard the gun emit a loud *POP* at the same time. The force of a sudden shock wave whammed into his body. His vision blurred. His muscles went limp. The last thing Arin felt was his kneecaps smacking the ground, then everything went black.

**IT WAS THE** same flood of images, but now they flicked by at a calm pace, like turning pages in photo album. Little Lia, torn dress and skinned knees, was up in the tree pelting rocks down with marksman-like accuracy. Then she was staring through the bars of the iron fence. Suddenly, her adult face was revealed from beneath her helmet. Shock and fear filled her eyes. Then, she was a young woman, screaming unheard words as tears streamed down her face. Her skin changed from soft and supple, to riddled with deep scars. His vision focused on one, another, seeing only the jagged slashes through her skin, until it traveled up to her face. She turned toward him with an accusatory fire in her eyes.

Arin's eyes snapped open. He lay still, taking in everything he had just experienced. Each image had not only been clear as day, but they had all carried with them the buzz of emotions that were, up until then, only memories. Even his most recent visions brought with them profound sensations he could only describe as shock and sadness. These weren't the same electrical pulses he experienced before but waves that rolled through him, producing physical effects with each peak and dip. How was that suddenly possible?

He allowed his eyes to wander, taking in his surroundings. The once fuzzy vent overhead came into focus. He sat up on his elbow. It was the same chamber, lit by the single lamp at its center. Arin's jacket had been neatly folded and placed under his head. Lia, now dressed in pants and a jacket, was curled up on the other side of the chamber with her back toward him. She was using the disdained dress as a pillow and seemed to be asleep. The long barreled gun was in a holster on her hip.

Arin crawled silently over to her side. He waited, watching Lia's slow breath to assure it remained steady, then he reached for the gun. His hand was a hair away when he heard the tell-tale click of a safety. Lia had produced another gun and had it aimed straight at his face. She twisted around to look him in the eye. "Do you really think I'd let my guard down so easily?"

"The last thing I remember was you shooting me," he said as he raised his hands. "It seemed wise to take the upper hand."

"You wouldn't have gotten it from that gun. This one on the other hand…." She gestured with the gun for him to get to his feet. She followed him up, holstered her second gun, and dusted off her clothing. "Shooting you was a security measure. It's only a particle pulse gun. It should disable your nanites, and their signal, for about two days. But since it's the only weapon of its kind, I will not hesitate to shoot you with my real gun if you try to take it again."

"You disabled the nanites? Entirely?" What he was experiencing now could only be described as utter disbelief.

"Yes. You're temporarily"—she gave him a once over as she thought of the best word to use—"vulnerable. So don't try anything too heroic, Commander. You might get hurt."

It explained everything but still seemed too impossible to be real. He examined his own body, searching for signs of change. One thing he certainly couldn't deny was the intense beating of his heart. Was that what shock felt like? He couldn't remember. Arin was still taking inventory, feeling for what could be actual bruises, when Lia picked up his jacket. Before he could snatch it back, she had put an incinerator to the fabric. It ignited and incinerated to dust in seconds. His commander's stars clinked to the floor.

"Why would you do that?" Impulse made him scoop up the tiny bits of metal.

"You'll never make it out of the badlands if you're recognized. Everything that identifies you as Unity has to go. Every stripe, every weapon, and every shred of your uniform."

She stepped back and gestured for him to disrobe. It was his turn

didn't allow it to linger long. "Now, if anyone asks, tell them we're"—she gave him a once over as she considered—"cousins. We've left Caldera City because of the occupation. We're here looking for work."

"And what happens if someone offers it to us?" She could see that he'd slipped into strategic mode and found herself feeling a tinge of respect for him as a soldier. She hid it beneath another casual response.

"Don't worry. There isn't any."

Now, with a plan in place and the prospect of a meal and a bed for the night, there was nothing left to do but wander into the valley and explore what lay ahead.

# FIVE

**ARIN MAINTAINED VIGILANCE** as they crossed the center of the village, noting each time they drew stares from the locals. For the most part, their appearance didn't seem too surprising to anyone, even though the notion of this part of the world being frequented by travelers seemed incredibly unlikely to him. Lia led them toward what he guessed was a tavern from the hand carved symbol of a frothy beverage hanging above the door. It made him wonder if anyone in the village could actually read. Luckily, he was wise enough to know not to ask.

Beyond the door, a crooked stone staircase lead down into a large stone room glowing with rainbow hues from a ceiling laden with stained glass lanterns. The few patrons inside lounged on low cushions and smoked from long hookah coils. There was calm and cheerful energy among them. Arin had just concluded that there were no apparent threats to monitor when Lia whispered, "Don't speak unless spoken to and follow my lead."

Suddenly, he was on edge again.

As they sat at a table in the corner, a barmaid in layers of swooshing fabric trundled up to them. "Why, you two are new to this village, ain't ya?" she declared with a warm smile.

"Just arrived. Came from Caldera looking for work." Lia responded with an even bigger smile and an accent that was an uncanny match to the barmaid's. "'Course all we need now is a good meal. Two full courses please." It all came rushing back to Arin in that instant. Lia loved pretending to be someone else. Alter ego's, she had called them, distinct personalities with their own life stories, accents, mannerisms, and odd little quirks to match. She had rarely gotten away with the act when they were children, since everyone in Waterford knew the good mayor's daughter, but she relished every opportunity she had to try on another persona. The previous seven years had clearly fine-tuned her skills.

"Well, I sure hate to be unwelcoming," the barmaid responded without the smile, even though her tone was just as jovial, "but I got to ask for pay up front, things being what they are these days."

"We don't have much money left," Lia responded with well-tuned humility. "But we did manage to leave with a little something." She pulled out a little burlap bag and handed it to the barmaid.

As she peered inside, her face lit up. Her smile remained. "Two full coming right up. And drinks are on the house." She scurried off, clutching the bag to her chest.

Arin didn't wait long before interrogating. "Have you been to this town before?"

"Nope."

"Then where did all that come from?"

"I know what people expect in this part of the world. So, that is what I give them. It's only when you deliver something unexpected that you start to raise eyebrows."

"And that bag? Are you carrying gold as well as a full arsenal?"

"Money doesn't get you very far out here. Wheat, on the other hand." As if punctuating her point, waiters delivered two full plates of food followed by two frothy, brimming steins. "Thank you much," Lia responded and immediately began to dig in.

Arin eyed the grayish mush and unidentifiable brown chunks. His meal's appearance was making his skin crawl. "They don't have fancy processors out here like they do in the city," Lia said as she shoveled down the gray mush. "But, it's still food. Eat up."

Arin weighed the prospect of another few hours without sustenance against that of swallowing the rubbery bits of over processed protein. He picked up a brown chunk, sniffed it. Lia snorted with contained laughter. "You're not helping," he responded, letting her laughter infect him.

"Don't worry. There's much better food where we're going."

It was the first mention she'd made of their secret destination. He could tell by the sudden tensing of her shoulders that it had been unintentional, but the door had been opened, so he attempted to step through it. "Which is where?"

"You'll know when we get there."

"Tell me now."

"I can't." She went back to shoveling down her meal in an attempt to cut him off.

"Why not?"

"Because it's too—"

Arin was sure she was going to say *dangerous* before she cut herself short. Her eyes were following a gaunt man who was rushing across the room toward them. Arin's hand instinctively reached for his missing gun. His posture stiffened as the man arrived at their table. Lia just smiled up at him, perfectly calm. The man wildly shook their hands in greeting, without saying a word.

The barmaid rushed over and slid up beside him. "You'll have to forgive Jakes," she explained. "He's been waiting for news from Caldera for weeks now." She turned toward Jakes and signed with her hands. "What did you want to ask them?" Jakes vigorously signed back. "I can't understand if you go so fast." She tossed her hands up in frustration and turned to Lia and Arin. "I'm sorry. We both just started learning so Jakes here could talk to everybody. It still takes us a minute to figure things out."

"Why would you need to learn so suddenly?" Lia's accent remained flawless, even in the face of this strange conversation.

"Oh, well, you see, Jakes here was a Mason in Caldera City." Arin was immediately alarmed at the mention of Mason. He turned his face away, his eyes down toward the table, and attempted to breath away a sudden rush of adrenaline. "They were putting up the biggest fight when them Unis took over," the barmaid continued. "Strikes and riots.

Got 'em too riled up, I guess. Jakes was talking back to one of them tin cans, so he decided to take away his ability to talk back." Jakes opened his mouth revealing the angry red stub where his tongue used to be.

Lia and Arin were both equally taken aback. Nonetheless, Lia directed her next words at Arin "Those heartless, hollow excuses for humans!" Jakes waved an angry fist in the air in agreement. Arin put a hand to his face, attempting to obscure his identity.

Jakes turned to the barmaid and signed. "No! Do you really think?"

"What is it?" Lia asked.

"He wants to know if that assassin that made it into Caldera City, killed the new leader."

Arin shot Lia a wary look from between his fingers. How could this isolated pocket of people know about that? The Unity would have done everything in their power to keep it under wraps. Even Arin's disappearance would have been covered up to maintain the illusion of constant and complete control. Somehow, all it took was one day and a traveler or tradesman from Caldera passing through this tiny oasis for the murmurs of truth to spread across the desert. What was far more disturbing to Arin was the barmaid's use of "that" when referring to the assassin. It was as if Lia's crime was not only a thing of legend but an act she had committed before. Then he spotted the sparkle of pride in her eyes and knew, without a doubt, that she had.

"That's what I heard," Lia declared and then leaned in to whisper in confidence "Can't say for sure because we had to sneak off in the middle of the night. But them Unis were sure torn up about something. Lots of commotion around the city center. They were looking for somebody for hours, but whoever it was up and disappeared."

Jakes jumped for joy and kissed the barmaid on the cheek. "I can't believe it!" she gushed. "All the way out here. We really are getting stronger, aren't we?"

"Sure are!" Lia agreed.

"That news calls for another round." The barmaid ushered Jakes off to help her get more drinks.

Arin waited until they were out of earshot, then leaned toward Lia.

"How many times have you done this?" he asked with the intensity of an interrogator.

"Just enough to stall the engines." She was almost flippant. "You and I both know it makes little difference. Caldera City is already under another hand. Of course, that's only because I missed." She was cold, ruthless. Arin had never seen this side of Lia before. He wondered how long it had existed and what had brought it into being. Arin leaned back and hid his face behind his hand again. Lia pulled it away. "Relax. No one will recognize you without your fancy wrapper on."

"You don't understand, the stonemasons—"

"Were your biggest annoyance, I know. I see now how you deal with such problems."

He'd had more than enough of her assumptions "My Guard never tortured anyone. I never would have allowed it."

"With or without torture, the illustrious Unity mission is to rid the world of these people. Mine is to help them believe that they can fight back and win."

Every fiber of his being wanted to argue, to shout down her zeal, to shame her pride, but deep in his core, he began to wonder if she was right. He felt himself on the verge of shouting, even if it was just for the sake of release, but he knew that even the slight raising of voices would draw too much attention their way. He put his strategist back in the driver's seat. "Then you can sit here and accept your anonymous accolades. I'm not going to stick around and start another riot."

Arin stood up, turned around, and found Jakes standing nose to nose with him, a full stein in each hand. He froze. Jakes stared at him, confusion in his eyes. Then, he smiled. Jakes shoved one of the steins into Arin's hand, clinked them both together, and took a swig of his. Arin relaxed his posture, forced out a smile, and raised his glass.

It was not long before Arin lost count of the number of glasses that had been handed to him, along with the hours that had passed while they were being imbibed. Whether it was through trust, or a desire to escape his company, Lia had given up on monitoring his behavior. She was standing by the bar in the midst of a rowdy conversation with a handful of locals. She concluded an unheard joke with a bawdy gesture, encouraging waves of raucous laughter. Her act was unflappable.

Arin felt a feminine hand gently trace across his chin in an attempt to direct his attention away from Lia and remembered that he, too, was in the midst of his own conversation. Three women, whose names he had instantly forgotten, had joined him at the table, pinning him into the corner. The oldest and probably most brazen woman, whose hand had assured his focus was on her, held his eyes. "I was saying… I just don't understand how such a strapping young gentleman as yourself wouldn't have been forced into build duty."

"I was, but we escaped in the middle of the night." He made no attempt at an accent but kept his responses short.

"How brave!" The drunkest of the women declared.

The young woman on his other side leaned in. "I heard that there are hardly any women left in the city. That they all got out first, headed for the mountains. Must have been terrible lonely."

He could feel her breasts against his arm. No, she was the most brazen on the three. "Perhaps," was the best response he could muster in his distracted state.

She pressed even harder against him. "You could always stay here. It's a very friendly community."

He felt a smile forming, but it was cut short by the clang of a kick against the table leg. Lia was standing on the other side, looking down her nose at Arin.

"We have to go now," she said curtly.

"Lia, hi. Have you met…?" Only then did he realize he had forgotten all their names, but Lia assured common courtesy was thrown out the window as she cut him off.

"Nice to meet you. We've got to go."

"Now?" It wasn't the argument he had wanted to have with her, but this was an opportunity to get it out of his system.

"Now."

"Why?"

"Yes, why?" the drunkest woman asked. The other two were staring daggers at Lia. She either didn't notice or didn't care.

"We just do," was all she said in response. Arin could tell he wasn't going to be able to press any further. He slid out of his seat and around the table to the serenade of all three women whining in disappointment.

They strolled through the silent center of the village. Lia didn't say another word until they were well away from the tavern. "We have a bed for the night. Actually, it's more of an old camel stall, but the camels died a while back, so the smell ought to be gone by now." Her tone was suddenly breezy. It annoyed him, so he decided to press her again.

"Bed? That was the only reason we had to rush out the door?"

"Can't turn down local hospitality."

"I don't think I would have," he admitted. She attempted to march off ahead of him, but he had seen her eyes roll as she took off. Suddenly, this was fun. Arin jogged to catch up, stepped into her path, and said, "Admit it."

"Admit *what?*"

She was curt again and didn't stop walking, but Arin kept pace with her, walking backwards so he could see her face. "You were jealous."

"Jealous?"

"That's right. This heartless, hollow excuse for a human actually had a good time tonight. And you couldn't stand it."

That brought her to a standstill. "Oh, so you suddenly remember what it's like to enjoy yourself? To smile and laugh and talk to other human beings as if you are one?"

"Yes." He wasn't attempting to get a rise out of her. It was the truth. She could see it too. All she could do in response was march off in silence again.

He tailed her, taking a moment to let it sink in. He had enjoyed himself. Every moment from the rush of adrenaline at the thought of being discovered for who they really were, to the feminine wiles being displayed for his benefit. There was something else, something deeper than the temporary thrill of those moments. That tavern had been brimming with the essence of camaraderie, buzzing with the sensation of human spirits bonding, and, for a brief time, Arin was one of them.

They reached the door of the camel stall and both stopped dead in their tracks as the acrid smell hit their noses. Lia attempted to breath only through her mouth. "Guess they were wrong about the smell."

"Are you sure this is a good idea?" Arin asked, but Lia was already digging through her travel pack. She pulled out the long barreled particle pulse gun and turned it on Arin. "Now, wait a minute," he said as she closed in on him.

"Why? If you enjoy having a good time, why should I stop you now? Or, did you forget that this was the only reason you were experiencing such sudden joy?" She was backing him into the camel stall as she spoke.

"You don't have to do this."

"Yes, I do, Arin. It's been two days, remember?"

She was right. Their safety was at stake if she didn't shoot him again. He wasn't sure if it was good or bad that he suddenly found himself standing near a pile of camel blankets. His landing would be soft but smelly. Either way, he wasn't looking forward to what came next. He decided he might as well enjoy those last few moments. "You just don't want to admit it," he said.

"What don't I want to admit now?" she asked, particularly annoyed this time.

"You wanted me all to yourself." Arin gave her a broad smile. Lia's eyes burned with indignance. He was still smiling when he heard the pop of the gun, then everything went black.

# SIX

**LIA DIDN'T HAVE** to hide how far Arin had managed to get under her skin. He was completely unconscious, and unconscious people don't gloat. She paced around him, muttering, "stubborn... egocentric... ass!" It did not alleviate her agitation. She wanted to kick him, to inflict as much pain as she could, even if he wouldn't feel it until he awoke, but even under duress Lia believed in fair play. She was still clear headed enough to check that all doors were closed around them before she shouted, "Why do you have to ruin everything?" That relieved enough of her tension for her to focus on arranging Arin's limp body into a comfortable position and placing a camel infused blanket under his head. She breathed out another wave of stress and dropped to her knees beside him. "You have no idea, do you?" she asked his unconscious form. It did not respond.

Lia fixed her eyes on Arin's peaceful face as she lay down beside him. Her gaze traced over his body, musing over every nuance of his appearance. So much had changed in the past seven years, yet so little. The man that Arin had become still showed hints of the boy he had once been. His bushel of thick hair was only in control now because of a military precision haircut. His nanite enhanced muscles were stretched, long and lean, over the body that had once been that of a gangly teenager. His hands were just as graceful, his profile just as distinctive.

Lia found herself reaching toward him. She had to fight the sudden urge to touch him, just to make sure it wasn't all an illusion. She froze in mid-air, then pulled her hand back and tucked it safely under her head. She watched his chest rise and fall, focusing on the steady rhythm of each inhale and exhale, until her eyes fluttered shut.

**BLOSSOMING INTO TEENAGE**-hood had not changed Lia's opinion of dresses. They were loathsome, cumbersome nuisances. She didn't care how many people told her what a lovely young lady she had become. In fact, it only made her loath that ridiculous ballgown even more. Then again, maybe it was because Arin was the only one who hadn't said anything complimentary about her appearance yet. She had just caught him staring off into the distance again. Where was his mind tonight? It didn't matter. She knew she would snap up his attention sooner or later.

Lia heard her father's not so subtle *"Psst!"* to get her attention and made the mistake of responding. As soon as she looked his way, he gestured for her to sit up straight and smile. She, of course, responded by slumping down further into her chair and turning away with a scowl on her face. He had been standing under that damn welcome banner all night, glad-handing the tin cans that had brought Waterford its very first nanite treatment center. She couldn't stand the silence any longer.

"I can't believe they're celebrating the opening of this thing. Even if the people in this town could afford injection, which they can't, they'll never set foot near this hospital again."

Her vociferous declaration only brought Arin half out of his stupor. "Isn't it about time our town caught up with the rest of the world?" he sighed out.

*That old argument again,* she thought. Snapping him out of it was going to require more extreme measures than usual this evening. She knew what to do. "Come on." Lia tugged at Arin's sleeve. "Let's have some actual fun." She didn't have to look back to know he was following.

Lia crossed the room, scanning the crowd as she strolled along. She settled beside the elaborate spread at the bar and tapped an impatient fingertip on its glistening top as she awaited her opportunity. As soon as all eyes were turned away, she scooped up a bottle of shimmering golden liquor and tucked it behind her back. Arin's eyes opened wide. That did it. He glanced around to see if anyone noticed her theft. She backed away, beckoning him to follow with a single seductive finger.

Once they were out in the darkened garden, she rewarded his compliance with a kiss, pulling his body up against hers. As soon as they came up for air, she dashed into the promised secrecy of a circle of planters, towing Arin along with her. She could hear the fabric of that damned gown scraping the stone of the planter as she hoisted herself up onto its edge. Good, she thought, knowing exactly what shade of fuchsia her father would turn as soon as she told him how it happened. She celebrated with a healthy swig from the bottle, then offered it to Arin. He took a furtive glance around the darkened garden as he took the bottle, then made a disgusted face as he swallowed back his sip.

"Papa never serves the good stuff for free," Lia explained "What do those tin cans know anyway? They couldn't get drunk if they tried." She downed another dose of the burning liquid and offered the bottle back to Arin. He shook his head. "Giving up already?"

"I was hoping we could talk." He was looking right in her eyes for the first time all night, but her mind had already moved on, hoping for other forms of attention now.

"We have the rest of our lives to talk." She plunked the bottle into the plants and pulled Arin toward her by his tie. She held him in an airtight kiss as long as she could, feeling him melt into her. It was working. She hooked one finger into his belt, inching him even closer. Then she tucked her hand under his jacket, gathered the fabric of his shirt into her fist and un-tucked her way from back to front. As soon as her fingers grazed the bare flesh on his side, he tensed up and seized her hand.

"Wait a second."

"What for?" She was still determined.

"If your father catches us, he'll hang me by my rented tie."

"Then we'd better take it off." As soon as her fingers wrapped around his tie, he snatched her other hand. "Why are you so antsy tonight?" she blurted out as she pulled both her hands out of his grip.

"I uh… I have something I've been meaning to tell you."

"Okay. Go ahead." Her patience had already reached its limit long ago, so when Arin took his time before uttering a word, she reached for the bottle.

He finally said, "I've decided to join."

Lia didn't even feel the bottle slip from her grip. She barely registered the loud smash of glass and the splashing of liquor over her feet. She stared at Arin in shocked silence.

"If someday I wanted to be a politician or a scientist or a doctor or anything really," he stammered "I would have to be a part of the Unity. If I join the forces now, then I can make it to the top, be the best at whatever I want."

"The best? What are you trying to prove, Arin?"

"This is the only way for me to control my future."

"You won't even be human anymore." Her voice was slowly raising as her shock was being replaced by anger.

"You don't know what I'd be like. You've never seen anyone whose been injected."

She could hear his doubt. It instilled her with hope. She could still argue this away. "I don't have to. Living without emotions is just wrong! What would make you any different from a machine? You won't be able to laugh or cry. You won't feel love."

"Or hate or fear!" There was suddenly no shade of doubt in his voice. "And I'll be stronger than I've ever been. Don't you realize what I'd be gaining?"

It became instantly clear. Arin, on the verge of adulthood, still wanted the same thing he had always wanted since he was a little boy, smaller and weaker than the others. Now, the weight of those selfish desires was crushing down on her heart. "Is that all that matters to you?" she asked in a whisper.

"I can't stay here forever. You were the one that told me not to be afraid. I thought you would understand."

She could feel the heat of fresh tears stream down her face. She couldn't stop them, but she still gathered enough strength of voice to say, "I do understand. You're still afraid. And you always will be."

She leapt off the planter, feeling the momentary tug as the stone tore her dress, but it did not slow her down. She ran, through the garden, past the noise of the party, into the darkened wing of the hospital, and down the long vaulted hall. She wanted to outrun her hurt, her rage. She wanted to race away from every grain of feeling she had ever had for Arin. She could hear him chasing her, matching her step for step, reaching out, ready to snatch her back. So, she just kept running, convinced that if she could outrun him, she could leave behind every moment they had ever shared. His steps petered out as he jogged to stop, but she did not slow down.

She was too far away to hear when he called out, "I love you."

**A RUSH OF** wind whipped sand around the starburst of stones. The light of dawn was just beginning to break, throwing a blue glow behind each billowing burst of sand. The heat of the day would calm the wind, but Corwin wasn't about to wait for that, and he certainly wasn't going to let a bit of sand stop him. He marched to the center of the starburst and stood by the flat stone at its center, glancing down, then out over the horizon, again and again, seeing nothing but the clouds of sand gathering, clumping, whirling, and disbursing again. The transport tossed another wave of sand up into the wind as it slid to halt beside the circle of stones. His sub-commander emerged but stood at a distance.

"Report." Corwin ordered with a shout as he continued to glance between the stones at his feet and what little he could see of the horizon line.

"Nothing, sir," she shouted back in earnest.

"Nothing?"

"Nothing north, west, east or south of this location. And our trackers haven't found a signal."

Corwin stomped toward her. "Two people, two dangerous Resistors, don't just disappear into nothing. You will find them, even if you have to turn over every rock in this wasteland."

"Yes, sir."

"Destroy this thing," he ordered as he walked off.

His sub-commander immediately responded, signaling their contingent to assist. Corwin watched as they picked apart and tossed away every stone in the starburst.

**THE MEMORIES THAT** flicked through Arin's mind throughout that night all involved one particular subject, sex. It wasn't too surprising, given the display of flesh that had been presented to him that evening, but it was not long before his most recent visions of the female form were replaced by his earliest. Vivid and visceral memories of Lia had come back with perfect clarity. It was true that every experience he had had in the interim had been less than memorable. Sex wasn't an unheard-of occurrence in a Unity soldier's life but certainly infrequent. None of them would have blamed the nanites for an apparent lack of drive, though Arin knew it had certainly had a hand in dulling the experience for him. Now, every memory from their first spark of intrigue in youth, to his first explorations of Lia's body played out as if he was reliving them. He could almost feel her.

Like anyone who had enjoyed their dreams, Arin attempted to sedate the urge to open his eyes as he felt himself returning to consciousness. He was also a bit afraid that Lia might be watching him, fully aware of her starring role in the sexual symphony that had played out in his mind. He rolled over and tried to hide his face, and his thoughts, in the blanket beside him. Then the smell hit his nose.

Arin jolted up to escape the acrid burn of camel stench. That's when the pain struck. A sudden, thunderous rush whammed against his eyes from inside his own head. It was worse than the smell. His eyes had not even fully focused, but one glance around the stall was enough to determine that Lia wasn't there. Arin pushed up to his feet and stumbled toward the door, hoping to leave both the smell and the pain behind.

The pain trailed along with him. His pulse generated a ceaseless thumping against his optic nerves as he wandered out into the village. Luckily, the light of morning had yet to break into the valley. He was sure that would have made it much worse. The villagers were commencing the business of the day, packing transport carts, feeding their animals, setting up street shops, and putting up shades against the coming sunlight. Those that acknowledged Arin did so with a smile and a friendly nod. No doubt their cover story had traveled throughout the village overnight. Arin wondered what else the locals might be saying about them.

The *put-put-put* of a laboring engine caught his attention. A cloud of dust revealed the approach of a beat-up old motorcycle with a dinged-up sidecar attached. Lia was in the driver's seat. She squeaked it to a stop beside Arin. "Isn't it great?" she asked with a bit too much enthusiasm.

Arin batted away the cloud of dust and exhaust fumes. "That's not exactly what I would call it." The sound of his own voice rattled around in his head. He wanted nothing more than to go back to sleep, camel stall or not.

"If you'd prefer to wait for better transport, then I can just go on and leave you here to take in a little of the local hospitality." She smiled up at him, one eyebrow raised. He was not amused. Lia slid off the bike, stepped up close to him, and whispered, "But you'd have to hope that the rumor I heard about the Unity Guard being in the desert this morning wasn't true." He could see the urgency in her eyes. He could also tell they were being watched by the villagers.

"I'm sure it's quite comfortable," he said, loud enough to both be heard by their onlookers and to generate an echo in his own brain.

"Hop in," she jauntily suggested.

"In the sidecar?"

"Were you expecting to drive?"

"Look at the size of that city. Look at the land around it. Lush. Sheltered. Do you think people would be living in craters in the desert if places like this were safe enough for them to go back to?" She could see him analyzing the scope of what lay ahead, calculating. The tactical approach was working, or so she thought, until he opened his mouth again.

"Are you're telling me a Resistance assassin is afraid of a handful of people with spongy brains?"

Now she was annoyed. "I didn't say I was afraid. I just said it wasn't going to be easy."

"If anything I heard about them is actually true, then they have no weapons. They just claw at people like feral cats. How dangerous can that be?"

"They don't need weapons. They swarm. You may be able to take down a few, but once they surround you, it's over. They'll take everything we have, and if we fight, they'll kill us."

He spent another moment calculating. "Then why go through that city at all?"

"Believe it or not, that's the safest way home." Lia was the one calculating now. She slid Arin's gun out of the holster under her jacket and turned it over in her hands as she thought. She looked Arin dead in the eye. "I need you to protect us."

"You mean I finally get my gun back?" His tone was joking, but she could see that he had slipped into soldier mode, so she laid out her instructions.

"Don't shoot anything unless you have to. They may come at us, but we'll be going faster. As long as we keep moving, we'll be okay. But if we stop, for any reason, then just shoot as many of them as fast as you can."

"Aye, aye, sir," he said as he reached for the gun. She pulled it back. He changed tack. "I won't let anything happen, Lia. I promise."

The sincerity of the promise was real. She passed over his gun, watched as he checked the ammo, the safety. It had slipped back into his hand like a missing appendage. She found that comforting. He gave her a subtle nod signaling his readiness. Lia started up the motorcycle again, and, after a few coughs of the engine, they began the descent toward the towering black ruins.

The sun was too low to break past the city walls by the time they entered. It was too late for Lia to go back and retrieve the thought of camping outside until dawn, which she had left unspoken at the city gates. Their only hope now was to find an entrance to the underground before the sun set altogether. Lia made it her sole focus, trusting that Arin's mind was entirely set on his task of protection.

The engine kept a steady *put-put-put* as they sped along, straight into the heart of the city. Dust clouded the air ahead, no doubt disturbed by several pairs of feet scampering into the shadows. The buildings became taller, the streets dark and narrow. A sudden flash of moment caught them both by surprise. Dark figures, shrouded in rags, darted out of the open and into the shadows. Lia kept her eyes on a continuous scan of streets, desperately seeking their escape. Arin peered down each narrow corridor they sped past, his aim at the ready, but each group of Scavs they came near scattered before they saw scarcely more than the whip of rags around a corner.

"They're running from us," Arin said without breaking his gaze down the barrel of his gun. "They're afraid."

"Don't assume anything." Lia had to shout over the overpowering drone of the engine.

"I know what I see. They're scattering like r—"

As if to defy Arin's assumptions, a crazed man flew out from behind a pile of rubble and grasped Lia by the hair. She screamed in agony but held tight to the handlebars. Arin took aim but fell off balance as the motorcycle swerved, smashing into one wall, then bouncing into another. Lia's scream was joined by Arin's cry of pain and the sizzling of searing flesh as he grabbed the engine to steady himself. He managed to push himself upright, shove the gun against the man's side, and shoot.

The crazed man's body bounced off the back of the motorcycle and rolled onto the street. Lia steadied herself, straightened the motorcycle, and sped up. "More will be coming," she warned as she revved the engine up to full speed and screeched the tires around the next turn. Arin breathed through the onslaught of pain radiating from his palm and wrapped it back around his other hand, steadying the gun.

Sunken faces and blood red eyes appeared in every crevice. The population of onlookers seemed to grow with every street they passed. Lia continued her scan as she drove the motorcycle toward an open square. As they zoomed out of the cloistered rows of buildings, the Scavs emerged with them. They ran across the field of flagstone, closing in on them from either side, like waves of locusts. Arin swept his aim across the crowd, but the motorcycle was overtaking their pursuers, so he reserved his shots.

Lia spotted their exit, but it was too late to make the turn. They were already speeding toward another narrow street when two Scavs stepped into their path. Lia didn't have to shout instructions. Arin dropped them both with two clean shots. Their bodies fell to either side of the motorcycle as it disappeared into another corridor of towers.

"I have to turn around." Lia shouted back to Arin.

"They're right behind us!" There was no changing that. They would have to drive straight through them. Lia pulled a hard u-turn, kicking up debris. The motorcycle came to a sudden stop. The engine ground and whined as she pushed the throttle. Scavs emerged from every crevice in the rubble and ran straight toward them. Arin spun around, shooting strategically in every direction, but there would soon be too many of them.

"Come on. Come on!" Lia willed the motorcycle back to life with a shout. The engine boomed, and they took off at full speed, leaving those Scavs in a cloud of dust.

More and more Scavs jumped out from every direction. They leapt at the motorcycle, clawing hands grasping at anything they could reach. They jumped in front, forcing Lia to ram right into them. The motorcycle jumped and jerked as it bumped over limbs. One of them grabbed the back of the motorcycle and was dragged along the street but did not relent. Arin kicked at the pale, gnarled hand holding tight until it lost its grip and disappeared under a trampling hoard of the Scavs.

The motorcycle zoomed back out into the open square. Scavs swarmed from every direction. Arin shot, one by one, taking down any that got too close, but there were too many to count. The swarm closed in fast. Lia drove straight toward her goal, a massive archway in the side of a building that was loosely boarded over. The long-fallen sign beside the archway announced is as Cassandra Station.

"We need to get underground." Lia pointed toward their only window of escape.

"This heap won't survive that!"

"Just hold on!" she screamed as the motorcycle flew at the boards, shattering them instantly, then slid down a staircase and slammed into a wall. *I should have listened to my own advice,* Lia thought, as she felt herself lift from the seat and fly over the handlebars, straight toward the wall.

Everything went black.

"Come on, Lia. Come back to me." Arin's voice was muted, the sight of him hovering over her came slowly into focus. She could also see the Scavs breaking through the rubble of the crash, seconds from being right on top of them.

She forced her impacted lungs to suck in enough oxygen. "Down. We have to go down." Arin scooped her up into his arms and ran down the staircase toward the darkness below. She watched over his shoulder as the Scavs broke through the rubble and reached desperate hands out toward them. Sound was quickly rushing back into Lia's ears, the hyena-like snarls of the Scavs, the crunching of debris under Arin's feet. They reached the bottom of the staircase and entered a large chamber, pitch black except for a single shaft of light shining through a grate above.

"Stop… *wait,*" Lia wheezed out. Arin placed her down in the pool of blue light and knelt beside her. They both stared up through the grate, listening to the chaos above. Sounds of scraping, twisting metal, and loud crashes mixed with the screams, snarls, and growls of the Scavs as they tore the motorcycle to shreds. The sounds slowly dissipated to distant whines and dull cracks as the last shaft of light disappeared.

Lia and Arin were left in total darkness.

**ARIN COULD TELL** Lia was trying to push herself up. He put an assisting hand on her back, felt as her lungs took in some spastic breaths, and then gradually calmed to a steady rhythm.

"They won't follow us down here," she said in a freshly strengthened voice, then began to fish around in her pack.

"Why?"

"They're afraid of this place." Lia clicked on a flashlight, revealing the staircase they had just descended. The debris field Arin had raced through turned out to be brittle human remains. They choked the staircase with a horrifying barrier of shattered bones. "After the Unity gassed the underground," Lia continued, "these tunnels never lost their reputation for being the biggest death traps this side of the world. Even the Scavs seem to remember that."

Arin was still transfixed on the gruesome sight as Lia got up to her feet. "You're telling me the Unity is responsible for that pile of bodies. Why would they kill all those people?"

"The tunnels were the underground network for the Resistance. It's how they passed supplies, information, weapons. When the Unity forces got too lazy to go around hunting down each individual Resistor, they just decided to kill them all at once. Those few who survived, well… you saw what happened to them." She gestured to the city above them with her light before swinging it into the tunnel.

Lia was busy searching their surroundings when Arin realized he was still holding his gun. He assured that she was looking away as he tucked it into his belt and hid it beneath his shirt. He stood up and glanced around, orienting himself. Lia's light bounced off the well-aged metal walls, producing a soft glow in the chamber. They were on a train platform, with tracks just below leading down a metal tube into darkness. Even in the dull spill of light he could still see the distinct shape of the human skeletons he had trampled to get them to safety. The sight made him feel sick. "These things, they happened during the first war. They happened when we were children, Lia. You can't hold me accountable for them."

She glanced over her shoulder. "If the uniform fits." She turned away and hopped off the platform, down onto the tracks. It was an attempt to end another argument before it began, but Arin was determined not to let that happen, not when he knew he could change her mind about him.

"Wait a minute." Arin hopped onto the tracks to pursue her in protest, but as his feet hit ground, he was struck by a sudden spasm of pain in his leg. He crumpled to his knees. Lia turned back and shined her light on him. He delicately pulled up his pant leg, revealing a large shard of wood embedded in his shin. "I didn't even feel that until now."

"And does it still hurt?" she asked.

Only then did Arin realize. "No. It doesn't." He opened up his palm to see that the searing burn he had just inflicted had almost entirely healed.

"The effects of the P.P.G. must be wearing off," Lia said, suddenly on edge. "We have to get moving."

Arin gritted his teeth, prepared to bear any unpleasant sensation, and yanked out the chunk of wood. He didn't feel the slightest hint of pain. The hole through his skin healed over, leaving just a trickle of blood behind.

Lia stared at what was left of the wound. "What does it feel like when you heal?"

"A little tingle. Not much else." Arin never did enjoy discussing his nanite enhanced healing with those who didn't possess it themselves. It made him feel like a sideshow attraction. Having been in the service of the Unity Army his entire adult life, he rarely had to. He rolled his pant leg back down, breaking her stare but not her fascination.

"What about when your injuries are worse? Like, when you get shot?" she asked.

"I wouldn't know. It's never happened." She gave him a bewildered look. "Is that so strange?"

"You're a Guard commander, a top tier target."

"To you, maybe. But I spent my whole life in Io City. There are no Resistors there. Everyone just—"

"Blindly follows orders."

"They have no reason to be unhappy."

"They have no ability to be."

Arin berated himself for having walked straight into that one. He couldn't think of anything to say in response. His attempt to change her mind about him would have to wait for another opportunity. Lia filled the silence. "Come on. This way." She walked off, headed down the tunnel into the unknown.

**LIA HADN'T EXPECTED** to feel such a lightness of spirit. Even with the end of their journey so close, the uncertainty of what lay ahead and the compounded exhaustion from everything they had experienced to get there should have weighed her down. Her flashlight produced nothing but a dot, dancing around in the darkness, providing only enough warning for them to know when they were about to face a scramble over debris. Their voices sounded small in the expansive space. They were facing a race against time, but somehow, those last few hours spent talking their way down the track made her feel like the carefree girl she had once been, the girl she had been when Arin was still in her life.

The subject of their shared past had come up again, but this time they spoke only of other people. "Danica James." That was the next name that popped into Lia's head.

"Probably married rich and has seven fat children by now," Arin responded. He searched his memory. "Lachlan Samson."

"Alcoholic," Lia declared, matter of fact.

"You say that about everybody."

"It's got to be true for him. I caught him trying to steal the bottles out of my father's liquor cabinet, more than once."

"You used to sneak sips of his golden."

"Yeah. But it was funny when I did it." Lia's eyes had adjusted well enough to see that Arin was smiling. How long would it last, she wondered. His injuries had already disappeared. Meanwhile, she was still feeling a sharp shock up her spine with every step they took and actively fighting the urge to curl up and go to sleep. She reminded herself that he could return to being a tin can at any moment, so she determined to make the most of whatever time they had left. She searched her memory for another name. "Logan Aaronson?"

"That one I actually know. He's the Assistant Counsel of Waterford."

"How?" she asked, incredulous.

"It only took him about five years to weasel his way to the top. I'm surprised you didn't hear about it. You really did just leave and never look back," he said, as if he was only just starting to believe her story.

She could feel him looking at her, with eyes probably enhanced enough to see every detail of her face. "I couldn't have gone back. Even if I had a reason." She picked up her pace in an attempt to escape his gaze.

"Of course, there is someone whose last few years are still a mystery to me," he called after her. "But I have a feeling there are some things she doesn't want to tell me."

Lia stopped, turned her light back toward him. "Like what?"

"How you got those scars." After scrambling his nanites, more than once, she wondered if he was going to remember seeing them at all. That same wrinkle of concern was on his brow, as if the recordings in his brain were playing that moment all over again. Strangely, she had no instinct to cut the conversation off, no desire to hide the truth from him. She allowed herself to replay her memories too.

"After I left Io City I was living, hiding really, in one of those towns way off the map. But a Uni bounty hunter found me anyway." She continued walking as she spoke. Arin followed close by her side. "He could have killed me, brought in my body. His payday would have been just as good, and it would have saved the Unis the trouble of trial with the same result. But that wasn't his style. He wanted someone to make an example of, to suppress the slightest hint of Resistance that my presence might have encouraged. So, he forced me into the town square, where everyone could watch, and stabbed me, seventeen times. Then he dropped me in the river. The last thing I remember was the water turning red."

It had been harder for her to say than she thought. She had to fight back the tears threatening to emerge. She breathed out, focused her eyes on the track ahead, and hoped that Arin was not looking at her face, but she could feel how close he was. "How did you survive?"

"I was saved."

"By who?"

"Someone with the means to save me." Remembering that part of the story helped to suppress her tears. It also reminded her of home and awoke her urgency to get back there. She could see Arin reaching for her shoulder from the corner of her eye but took off at a brisk pace, leaving his hand hovering in the air.

A wall had collapsed across the tracks ahead, blocking their view of what lay beyond. Lia assessed the best climbing path with her flashlight, then stepped up to begin her ascent. The rubble under her foot gave way. She felt the pull of gravity threaten to send her flying back onto the tracks, followed by the sensation of Arin's hand snatching her wrist, pulling her upright, and steadying her on her feet again. He was standing on the pile beside her, one arm wrapped around her back, the other still grasping her wrist. Once she recovered her breath from the alarm of nearly falling, she managed to utter, "Thanks."

She tried to take another step up, but Arin held on to her. She turned to look at him and found herself able to trace his features in the darkness. A look of concern and empathy was in his eyes, but this time it did not snap away in an instant. He released her wrist and ran his hand over her cheek.

The feeling of his skin touching hers melted away all other sensation. There was suddenly no pain, no exhaustion. Lia closed her eyes and let herself feel the electricity from his fingertips. The warmth of his body, the sound of his breath, drew closer, closer. It wasn't until she felt the sensation of his lips nearing hers that reality of their present came crashing back into her mind. Her eyes snapped open. She pulled out of his arms. "We have to keep moving."

Lia turned away and began climbing up the pile of rubble. She hadn't said anything more. She hadn't waited for his response. She hadn't even looked him in the eye. She knew she couldn't until the sensation of his hand on her cheek was too distant for her memory to recreate. She listened to him climb up behind her, scramble down the other side, and drop onto the tracks again. They continued on in silence.

Lia wasn't sure how long it had been. The artificial night they traveled through had robbed her of all sense of time, but the need to walk just ahead of Arin had kept her moving fast enough for her feet to be numb to the impact of each step. No matter how safe they were underground, she dreaded the thought having to stop now. So, she pressed on, step after dead step. After a sharp turn in the tunnel, they emerged at a junction where several tunnels converged. In one of the narrow tubes ahead, a distant light flickered.

"Finally!" Lia exclaimed. Adrenaline, fueled by relief, pushed her into a run. Arin's footsteps kept a steady pace with hers as she ran toward the light. They jogged deeper and deeper in, becoming surrounded by more and more flickering lights. The eerie glow revealed a series of small green doors lining the tunnel walls ahead.

Lia skidded to a halt and scanned the doors, silently counting to herself. She approached what she guessed to be the correct door and felt the bricks surrounding it. One of the bricks rocked in place. Lia experienced another spike of excitement. Home was so close now. She pulled out the brick and reached into the hole it left behind. After a short struggle with her shaking fingers, a latch came loose. The door swung open.

Lia placed the brick back and prepared for Arin's inevitable questions, but he said nothing. Whether it was due to injury, exhaustion, or the shock of his attempt to kiss her, Lia had not thought of what to say when they arrived. As she turned back toward him, she decided to let her instinct take over.

"I need you to trust me." These were the only words she could grasp a hold of.

"Where are we?" His strategic mind was switching on, pushing him to prepare for whatever lay ahead.

Lia let her instinct speak for her again. "Once we go through this door, it may seem like... I told you I would help you, and I will. You just have to believe that."

She prepared for an argument, but he simply said, "I do." Every aspect of his being, the straightness of his back, the steadiness of his hands, the unflappable trust in his eyes, indicated that it was true.

Lia had nothing left to say, so she pushed open the door and led Arin through to the other side.

# EIGHT

**THEY WERE UNDER** some kind of immense structure. Bundles of conduit, hanging from the ceiling, followed a straight hallway toward an unseen end. The air hummed with electricity. Arin instinctively switched his senses into overdrive. His eyes scanned for any movement. His ears listened for the hint of any sound. He kept one hand running along the wall, feeling for heat, vibration, moisture, anything that would indicate what kind of building they had entered. He kept his other hand poised, ready to snatch up his hidden gun. He could tell the impact of the crash had rattled Lia more than she admitted. He was sure that if she weren't compromised in some way, she would have remembered that he still had his gun. He told himself that keeping his hand at the ready was only to help protect her if need be. It had nothing to do with trust.

The end of the hall soon revealed itself to be a lit room, producing a perfect rectangle of white light ahead. Arin could hear the mumbling of voices. Lia seemed to be preparing herself. She straightened up, breathed in deep, and marched toward the light. Arin placed his hand on his gun and followed. They had not gone more than a few steps when loud alarms blazed into the hallway. The deafening sound bounced around the metal walls. They both shielded their ears, but when armed guards began racing toward them, Arin pulled out his gun and took aim.

*"No!"* Lia screamed, barely audible against the klaxon alarms. She shoved his arm aside. His shot fired off center and zipped into the lead

guard's shoulder. The guard crumpled against the side of the hallway. The others flooded past him as if he were nothing more than debris in their path. Lia yelled as they approached, but her voice was drowned out. She stood in front of Arin, preventing him from taking aim as the guards closed in and surrounded them.

Arin was thrown to the ground by the force of four guards. Another two pushed Lia to one side and pinned her against the wall. The gun was ripped from Arin's hand, a blinding punch delivered to the bridge of his nose, but he fought back. Lia continued to yell, desperately trying to be heard. A series of lights clicked on down the hallway. The alarm suddenly silenced.

"Stand down! *Now!*" Lia screamed. The guards holding her immediately retracted in embarrassment.

"I'm sorry, Sub-Commander," one of them stuttered, popping to attention. "We didn't realize."

"All of you stand down. Now," she said in a firm voice directed at the four guards keeping Arin pinned to the ground.

"The tracking alarms went off. He's got to be—"

"He is. I'm the one who brought him here, and I'm ordering you to release him." The guards immediately released all four sets of hands, allowing Arin to push back up to his feet, but they held his gun captive and kept theirs aimed toward him. Lia did not order them to do otherwise. They were calling her sub-commander, but of what army? Of how many? Why hadn't she told him? The guard that took the bullet gave a groan of displeasure from his seated position against the wall. He was close to passing out. "You two take him to the medical lab," Lia ordered "The rest of you take us to the commander."

Arin felt the point of two guns stick into his back and shove him forward. Lia took up position ahead of him and marched off. She did not say another word. She did not even look back. The answers to his questions would have to wait.

They ascended one set of stairs after another. The featureless concrete treads eventually became shiny marble, surrounded by elaborately carved balustrades. Up and up they continued. The march of booted feet was softened by plush carpeting. Arin glanced upward and could see the staircase winding up several stories above. The structure was old, grand, immense in scale, and, judging from its highly guarded entrance, extremely well-fortified.

On one of the softly carpeted landings, they veered away from the staircase toward a large set of double doors. Lia pushed them open with authority. The room on the other side was oversized and opulent. Mirrors lined one wall, bouncing light up toward the ornate ceiling. Tall windows, covered in thick drapes, lined the other wall. Across the room, a matching set of double doors swung open. A striking and formidable man, older and with a notably larger stature than Arin, charged into the room.

"Roland." Lia called out to him. His face changed as soon as he saw hers. The burning look in his eyes melted away, his firm jaw softened with a smile. Lia raced into his arms. Arin was forced to a stop by the guards and surrounded on all sides. From where he stood, he had a clear view of Lia and Roland as they shared a passionate kiss. He held her face in his hands, keeping her close. Arin attuned his eyes to their lips and ears to their whispered conversation.

"I knew you would be all right." Roland said to her. "I never doubted for a moment."

"I am. I promise." Lia assured. Then her voice changed. Arin could hear the waiver of doubt. "But there's something I need to explain."

That's when Roland turned his eyes toward Arin. His jaw hardened again. His burning stare returned. "He's Unity?" he asked Lia over his shoulder as he approached Arin.

"He is." Lia admitted. "He managed to capture me after the assassination, but he didn't turn me in. He saved my life, Roland."

"An admirable task indeed. But I don't see cause to have brought him all the way here." He was speaking to Lia but without breaking his gaze on Arin. He looked him up and down, assessing.

"They were going to review his recordings. They would have seen me, seen my face. Then, they would have executed him. We can't let that happen. Not after what he did for me."

Arin had kept his eyes on Roland as Lia explained. The use of the word "we," the implication that he owed as much to Arin as she did, had made him angry. Lia had been so focused on pleading her case that she hadn't noticed. Roland stepped toward Arin. The guards silently stepped aside, clearing his path. Arin straightened up, taking a soldier's posture, prepared for anything.

"Name and rank?" Roland demanded.

"Timothy James Arin, Commander, Elite Guard."

"A commander nonetheless." That made him even angrier. "Tell me then, Commander, why would a soldier of your rank decide to spare the life of someone he knew to be a Resistance assassin?"

Lia flicked Arin a wild-eyed look from behind Roland. It wasn't until that moment that he realized, this man into whose arms Lia had raced had not so much as flinched when Arin told him his name. He had no idea who Arin and Lia had once been to each other. He had never even heard his name before. Panic was overtaking Lia's countenance. She hadn't prepared either a softening way to tell him the truth or a harmless lie to cover it up. So, Arin provided one for her. "She's my cousin."

It was the simplest, least considered, and yet most assured lie Arin had ever told. It threw Roland off. He glanced back at Lia. Her face snapped from panic into abject sincerity. "He's the only family I have left. I couldn't let that go."

It was a flawless response, so convincing, so sincere. Arin wondered if Lia's influence over the last few days had made him better at lying or if it was his protective instinct that had suddenly instilled him with this unexpected gift. He didn't have the benefit of seeing Roland's face, of assessing whether or not the lie had worked when he responded. "I would never ask you to." His tone darkened. "But I can't have a Unity commander in my stronghold."

"We can change that," Lia said excitedly. "I told him I would bring him here to remove the nanites."

"Wait! What?" Suddenly Arin's protective instincts were focused solely on his own needs.

"You said you would do it permanently if you could. That's the only way," Lia explained from a distance.

"You never told me that's what you were planning. I never agreed to that!" Arin yelled. In the shock of that reveal, he had forgotten he was surrounded by armed guards. He stepped toward Lia and was instantly frozen by the click of safeties being pulled back all around him. As his focus shifted back to Roland, he found himself staring straight down the barrel of his gun.

"You should have gotten your story straight before you came through that door. Until you do, you remain a threat, and you will be treated as such." Arin looked into Roland's eyes, steadfast, unflinching. He could swear he saw Roland's finger inching toward his trigger. Then he dropped his aim and instructed his guards. "Take him to the cage."

Roland proceeded to march back in the direction he had arrived from, sweeping Lia along with him. The guards spun Arin around and forced him out the other way. He dared to look back before they cleared the threshold. Lia was also looking over her shoulder as Roland pulled her away. They shared one last glance with each other before disappearing beyond opposite doors.

LIA PREPARED TO be yelled at, accused of betrayal, or simply ignored. However angry Arin might be at this moment was completely justifiable in her eyes. Then again, she thought, he might feel nothing at all. The second day since she had last shot him with the P.P.G had dipped into night. There might be nothing left within him that was even capable of anger. She also prepared to meet with the shell Arin had become.

As she approached the guard at the door, he both came to attention and squirmed with discomfort at the same time. Lia knew at once that Roland had ordered him not to let anyone in, even her, but she was their superior, too, and she always got her way. She cut off his attempt at a greeting. "You know what I want. You know I will order you to comply, and you know that you will. You have my assurances that I'll take full responsibility with the commander for your breach of orders. As long as you don't waste my time." It didn't take long for him to make up his mind. He unlocked the door, stepped aside, and let her through.

The small room beyond the heavy door was divided in half by a floor to ceiling metal grate. Arin was on the opposite side of the grate, pacing like a trapped animal. *Not quite a tin can yet,* Lia thought. If anything, his body language indicated an overabundance of emotions. The guard clunked the outside latch shut behind her. Arin stopped pacing and approached the grate. She wasn't ready to look him in the eye, so she examined the contents of his cage as she walked toward him. There was a small cot, utilitarian at best, but on top was a tray of fresh food and a folded pile of clean clothing. Lia was relieved to see she had had at least some influence over his current circumstances. She finally looked up.

They stared at each other in silence through the crisscrossing iron. The anger was there, the hurt of betrayal, but there was something else. Arin's eyes were searching hers for answers. More than anything, he just wanted to know the truth. It made Lia feel heartless for ever having kept it from him. She was suddenly compelled to tearfully share her entire life story with him, but she reminded herself that at this moment, in this place, she was a soldier, and she had to act like one. She stifled her guilt and began to explain. "I couldn't tell you where we were going."

"Of course not. It wouldn't have been that easy to get me here if I knew I was walking into a trap."

"This isn't a trap."

"What do you call this then?" He shook the iron grate, sending a loud rattle around the room.

"Luxury accommodations compared to where you could be." The jolting sound had ignited Lia's instinct to argue. "If it were only up to Roland, you'd be in a box with no bed, no clothes, no food, nothing. This is where you want to be."

"Then where am I? And who, exactly, is Roland?"

"You're in the stronghold of the underground Resistance Army. Roland is our commander and... my husband."

Arin stepped back. He looked down at the ground as he absorbed this information. Lia actively fought against the desire to keep talking, to confess any and every truth that popped into her mind.

"So, I'm a prisoner of war?" he asked without looking up.

"Not if I can help it." He didn't budge. He wasn't buying her assurances anymore, so she quickly added, "And not if you let us remove the nanites."

"Is that why you brought me here? To turn me back into Tiny Tim?" He finally looked up but with accusation in his eyes.

"You asked for my help, and I want nothing more than to help you. I swear. This is the only way." She was pleading, begging for him to show some grain of trust in her, but his strategic mind had taken over, preventing anything else he might be feeling from surfacing.

"You can't do it, not without killing me. And it's not as if you haven't had ample opportunity to do that already."

"Yes, we can. You have no idea who you're dealing with here."

"Someone with the means to save me?" he coldly asked.

Lia hated having her own words thrown back at her, but she was still more compelled to get him to believe her than to protect her pride. "More than you know." She couldn't tell whether or not he believed anything she had just said. "Careful what you tell him. He knows where I grew up, who my father was... a lot."

"Obviously not everything." The accusation was in his eyes again.

"Not the things I was trying to forget, no." His look of accusation suddenly dissipated into abject emptiness. Was he hurt by her words, or had his nanites simply switched back on at that exact moment? She waited for something else, some sign of anger, of acceptance, even a hint that his mind might be calculating his next move, but there was nothing in his presence at all. Lia had no way of knowing how Arin felt about being erased from her past.

The door latch clacked. Lia knew it couldn't be anyone but Roland. She backed away from Arin and turned toward the door as it swung open. Roland didn't attempt to hide his annoyance as he walked in. Lia was quick to pacify him. She stepped in close, put her hands on his chest. "I had to come talk to him. He had no idea what he was walking into."

"Nor should he have. Just leave the explaining to me." It was a firm order, but Lia didn't budge. She looked up into his eyes, wearing her worry on her face. After a moment, he softened against her touch, put his hands on her shoulders, and gave them a gentle squeeze. "You said yourself you had a hard journey." His voice was warm. "Rest now."

That request, she didn't refuse. She nodded and left Arin alone with Roland.

**ARIN TOOK A** proud chinned posture as Roland approached. He understood how this was going to work. He had studied every great strategic mind of the century. His training was more than thorough. He knew the benefits of being a cooperative P.O.W., so he intended to demonstrate that he was.

"Lianna told me what happened," Roland began. "She's attempting to convince me that we don't need to have this conversation through a cage. Of course, I'd be a lot easier to convince if I didn't have a guard with a bullet hole in his shoulder."

"That was instinct. I apologize."

"It was as much her fault for forgetting to disarm you. Nonetheless, you're lucky you missed, both my guard and my wife." Cooperative or not, Arin still had to contend with Roland's anger. That was not a barrier Unity training had prepared him to surmount.

"There are still a few things I'm trying to piece together." Roland paced as he spoke. "What made you decide to be a Unity soldier?"

The question threw Arin for a loop. What did this have to do with Lia, the assassination, their escape? He would just have to play along to find out. "I wanted to be a part of the greatest scientific achievement in the history of mankind." Arin answered with confidence.

"I've heard that one before." Roland said, dismissively.

"The Unity represents progress toward a better future."

Roland nearly laughed. "Don't quote me propaganda."

"I believe in embracing any opportunity to better the world, the human race... and myself."

That answer brought Roland's pacing to a standstill. He looked Arin in the eye, judging his sincerity. "Perhaps we're not so different, after all."

That's when Arin realized it had just been a mind game. Roland was trying to draw him out, to get him to reveal his true self, and with that, any degree of weakness. Arin's facade refused to waiver, but inside he chastised himself for falling for it.

Roland's next question threw another spanner into the works. "By choosing to protect Lianna, you've sacrificed everything. Why?"

It was a straight question, and, by answering it honestly, Arin knew he would be the one drawing Roland out, so he told him the truth. "She's the only person left from a past I thought was long out of my reach. I couldn't let that go."

Roland's eyes burned with intensity. "Interesting." It was his only response, but it revealed everything to Arin. Roland's weakness was Lia. Roland broke their eye contact all at once. "You'll be safe here," he said as he headed for the door. "The trackers that traced your signal coming in also prevent it from sending out, and you're as far away from any Unity encampment as you can get." He paused and, without turning around, added, "You can join us for breakfast in the morning. It's what she would want."

There it was again, the glimpse of a man who would do anything for his wife. Arin almost wanted to gloat, but he had not forgotten the necessities of good conduct when one is under his enemies' thumb. "Thank you."

Roland exited, the latch clacked shut, and Arin was, once again, alone in his cage.

**ROLAND TOOK HIS** long climb from the basement to the tower in stride. He needed time to collect his thoughts. The days spent wondering what had happened to Lianna when she didn't return on time, assuming the worst, then actively suppressing those dark thoughts, refusing to let them twist away his sense, had been hard enough. Now, to have the joy of her safe return coupled with the unanticipated and unwelcome burden she willfully brought into his home, his sanctuary, had rattled his mind. It was worsened by the fact that he knew, beyond any doubt, that she was hiding something from him.

Since the moment they met, Lianna had never lied to him, but when it came to allowing gaps in her stories—black holes where the truth was something she chose not to share—she was a master. She had laid out the events surrounding the assassination and the details of their arduous journey back in such complete and colorful detail, that Roland knew she must be compensating for the information she was omitting. He wouldn't ask her what that was. He also knew, too well, that seeking out the truths she had cloistered in her mind was like coaxing an animal out of its burrow. If promised peace and safety, it might choose to emerge, but if actively pursued, it would only dig deeper.

As he reached the carpeted staircase his footsteps fell silent, and the sudden quiet brought another chilling recollection racing to his mind. "I couldn't let that go." They had both said it about the other. A word for word repetition, not of a rehearsed lie, but of a steadfast truth, equal in importance to both of them. What is it they have both chosen to hold on to?

Roland's suspicious mind had become accustomed to racing through every possible conclusion and then quickly eliminating the unlikely. He also always retained the most ludicrous outcome as a possibility knowing that, when desperate, humans will often engage in the most ludicrous of behaviors. It was an effective, and well-practiced, technique for figuring out his opponent's next move. He had just started this familiar process when he brought his mind, and his climbing, to a dead stop. He refused to analyze his wife as he would his enemy. He quickly erased all the possibilities that had already written themselves in his mind and replaced them with one simple statement.

*She came home to me.*

He shook the last of his thoughts loose, letting them melt into the corners of his mind, as he ascended the final flight toward their bedroom. Lianna was standing by the open window, letting the night air flow through her dressing gown. Roland gave himself a moment to imprint this image in his memories as he repeated to himself the truth that he wanted to prevail over all others. She came home to me.

She turned and smiled, melting away the last few stray thoughts that had refused to leave his mind. Seeing her now finally brought him some peace. "I thought you'd be asleep," he said as he closed the door.

"I waited for you."

He began to take off his shirt as he walked into the room. She was by his side in an instant, wrapping her arms around him. Roland felt her cold fingertips trace down his spine and settle into the small of his back. She held her body against his, seeming to need his warmth to help melt away her own chilling thoughts. Roland absorbed the moment. He traced his hands over her hair, down her shoulders. He felt himself graze the bandage on her arm and retracted his hand on instinct.

"It's already healing," she said without breaking her hold on him. "Faster than I thought possible."

The mention of her gunshot wound instantly reminded Roland of his torturous days in wait for her return and that the man who inflicted it was now in a cage in his basement. He peeled her arms from around his waist and stepped back. He had to speak of other things to reset his mind. "It's getting too dangerous at the border for me to send you out again."

"Aren't I always the best soldier for the job?" she asked with a cheeky smile on her face.

"Glad to see it hasn't gotten to your head." He returned her smile. "But you're just one person, against an army whose numbers increase daily. And one of them did catch you this time. Who knows what could happen the next?"

She pulled away and turned her back on him. She must have considered that an insult. She probably assumed he was disappointed in her. Perhaps she could tell that he, indeed, was. He reminded himself to tread lightly with his next words. "I assume you have another plan in the works then?" she asked without turning around.

"I do."

"And will you tell me what that is?"

"When the time is right."

"Yes, Commander."

It was going to take more than soft words to make up for his slip. He wrapped his arms around her, pulled her back gently. "You don't ever have to call me that in this room."

"Just trying to follow orders, sir."

"That's a first," he said.

She let out a little laugh, making it clear he was back on her good side. He could feel her relaxing into his embrace. He nestled himself into the soft nape of her neck, breathed in her smell, and reminded himself of the only truth that mattered.

*She came home to me.*

# NINE

**CORWIN DIDN'T MIND** the dressing down. He knew his discovery would make the counsel want to eat her words. He stood, straight and proud, across from her desk as she tapped her admonishment out with drumming fingers. "How am I supposed to tell who the real traitor is when my new commander can't seem to deliver the same fugitive?" she asked.

"They didn't disappear on their own. They were helped by more Resistors than we even know are out there. When we find those two, I guarantee we'll drag out a whole nest of them." Corwin was silenced by the raising of a single finger.

"Do not feed me conspiracy theories, Commander," she snapped back. "They don't explain away your incompetence."

The perfect opportunity to turn her around had arrived. "Then feed on this," Corwin said as he threw the little burlap sack of seeds onto the counsel's pristine desk. He relished the moment of silence that followed as she plucked out some of the seeds and rubbed them between her fingers. "How many people on the fringe can pay for their drinks with real wheat? We find out where those seeds came from, we find their hideout."

She bit into a seed, confirming its authenticity. That was all it took to gain her trust. "What do you need?"

"Long range transport and a legion of front-men."

The counsel didn't hesitate. "Be ready to leave by dawn."

"Yes, Counsel."

Corwin saluted and turned to leave, but she held him back with that same powerful finger. "Commander Corwin, should you return empty handed again, I will be forced to call in our top tracker. Do *not* make that necessary."

Corwin couldn't believe what he was hearing. How could he be accused of spreading conspiracy theories and then threatened with replacement by the very originator of Resistance conspiracies himself? At least she showed very little interest in bringing Martrim into the picture. No one in their right mind wanted that maniac around.

"You have my guarantee there will no cause to bring Sub-Commander Martrim out here. My Guard is more than capable of controlling a few border pests."

She spilled the seeds out of the little burlap sack and spread out the pile, musing over their mysterious origin. "And the town where you found these?" she asked without looking up.

He straightened up as tall as possible before answering. "Firmly under our control, Counsel."

The counsel looked up and nodded. She may not have eaten her words, but she had swallowed back enough of them to satisfy Corwin. He marched off and began his preparations to return to the hunt for his fugitives and whatever allies were at their side.

He would find them. He was certain of it.

**ARIN USED THE** long—and very well escorted—walk from his cage, up the winding staircase, to stretch out his spine. He hadn't so much slept on the small cot, as spent the night waiting for his nanites to return to full functionality. He wasn't entirely sure it had happened. His injuries had healed, and all other physical discomforts were minimal to nonexistent, but without the benefit of another person to test his emotional state, he had no way of knowing if his system had completely normalized again. There was no one moment, no sudden sensation, or lack thereof, to indicate that anything had changed. He had actively tried to hold on to the emotional effects of the particle pulse gun for as long as his will allowed. It must have worked, for at least a little while, be-cause his injuries were long healed by the time he felt the overwhelm-ing need to kiss Lia in the tunnel, followed by the painful sting of her rejection. He had tried, and failed, to conjure up the same emotions through memory, but they hadn't been nearly as intense. Perhaps his nanites were back to normal, or perhaps those feelings were bound to Lia's presence and impossible to create without her.

Arin's night spent staring up at the ceiling and listening to the resounding silence had brought him to at least one determination. He was *not* going to be put back in that cage.

His armed escorts led him to the same set of double doors and into the same grand room he had been in the previous night. Early morning sun was spilling through gaps in the long curtains, forming slits of bright light across the slick floor. One of those slashes of light fell across a broad table in the center of the room. An elaborate spread of fresh fruits, cured meats, cheese, and bread was laid out on the table. Arin was ungraciously shoved to a halt a few paces away and made to wait in silence with his charming company.

The doors across the room swung opened, and Roland marched in. "You're dismissed," he said without even bothering to glance up in the guards' direction. They responded so quickly that Arin felt the wind as they rushed past him. His first thought was that, in their ab-sence and with his system presumably at full strength, Roland would not present a challenge to him.

Then he noticed Roland's weapons—a simple six-shooter in a holster on one side of his belt and a large hunting knife with an elaborately-carved handle on the other. Arin was weighing up the potential damage those relatively mild weapons might do to him as Roland approached. When he finally looked up into Roland's eyes, he could tell he had been doing the same thing.

Neither of them seemed to have come to a decisive conclusion.

Roland came to a standstill behind the chair at the head of the table. "Lianna will be with us in a moment."

Having not been invited to move, Arin chose not to. His eyes scanned the colorful feast laid out on the table. "The food, is it all real?" he asked.

A spark of pride lit up in Roland's eyes. "Every last bit of it, farmed just outside these walls."

"Huh." That short response had left Arin's mouth before he had a chance to think better of it. Perhaps his system was not entirely back to normal yet.

"Surprised?" Roland asked.

Arin choose his next words carefully. "I just didn't expect to see such bounty out here on the fringe."

"And why is that?"

"I've seen nothing but small villages, destroyed cities. No organized industry to speak of."

Roland gripped the back of the chair. "You've seen only what the Unity would have you see, what they would have you believe. That the people who choose not to join their society lack the ability to know any better. That the Resistors spend their lives in an ignorant haze, scrambling to survive. It's time to open your eyes, lest you make another declaration without the knowledge to back it up." One of Roland's gripped hands formed a pointed finger and aimed firmly toward the window. Arin hated the idea of turning his back on a man with a gun, especially one he had just unintentionally angered, but he was still playing the cooperative prisoner. He marched toward the window and parted the curtains.

His eyes didn't take long to adjust to the blaze of sunlight, and he found himself facing a long balcony connecting each of the tall windows and wrapping around a massive structure. He stepped out and was immediately confronted by a dizzying drop. Beyond the rows of trees immediately below, collections of small buildings formed a city larger than Caldera, which expanded across the landscape and met with tidy farmlands at the horizon. Roland stepped out onto the balcony. Arin whirled around to face him.

"Welcome to Cambria," Roland said with that same spark of pride in his eyes. He pointed down toward the foothills surrounding the grand structure. Square wooden cabins filled a bald patch of land, which swarmed with men and women, all sparring and exercising. "That is the army your leaders would have you believe no longer exists. This is the way of life and the land they would all die to protect. I would not underestimate us again if I were you."

Roland ducked back inside, leaving Arin to take in his surroundings. As unexpected as Cambria's appearance was, it did not stop Arin from assessing whether or not he could take the impact of a leap over the balcony. He thought better of it and went back inside.

Arin marched himself to the opposite head of the table, mirroring Roland's position. "And where, exactly, is Cambria?"

"A place on the map your leaders are woefully ignorant of."

"I was told there was nothing but sparse townships on this side of the world. No farms, no cities. And it wasn't an elaborate lie. The Unity wouldn't keep information about a place like this from the commanders they would expect to secure it for them. How can they not know this exists?"

Roland smiled. It was obviously just the type of interrogation he had been hoping for. "The Unity's greatest strength is also its greatest weakness. The technology that makes them virtually indestructible encourages the continued belief that they are." At that moment, the doors opened, and Lia hurried into the room. She slowed her approach as she crossed into the thick cloud of tension hovering between Arin and Roland. He gestured toward Lia with an open arm. "It hasn't even crossed your leaders' minds that the last five officials assassinated were all killed by the same person."

"Seems I'm a bit late," she said, attempting a casual air as she reached Roland's awaiting hand.

"More than a bit," Roland muttered to her under his breath, though it was loud enough for Arin's ears.

"Five?" Arin asked. He wasn't done interrogating yet. Lia hesitated.

"That's just the counsels. There are more than a few others under her belt," Roland proudly answered for her, concluding his statement with a kiss to the back of her hand.

Arin eyes flicked from their clasped hands up to meet hers. "So, that's your specialty," he said, holding her gaze.

She turned her eyes down toward the table, so Roland chose to answer for her again. "Lianna is the sub-commander of our sharpshooter team, our city Guard, and our highest level assassin. Especially skilled at taking out Guard commanders and the like."

"Guess I'm lucky I caught her first." Arin had spoken without thinking again and clearly with the motivation of crushing Roland's pride. He definitely wasn't back to his emotionless, strategic self quite yet. Arin and Roland entered a silent stare-down.

The broad wooden doors swung open once again, and a well-dressed man, bearing the same armaments as Roland, waltzed into the room.

This time Lia was the one who muttered, "Perfect timing."

**ROLAND TURNED TO** see who had entered and knew immediately why Lianna had been late. He attempted to shut down whatever she was trying start up. "I don't recall inviting *you,*" he snapped.

"I did," Lianna retorted. At least she wasn't trying to hide anything, Roland thought.

"And who am I to give up the chance for a fine meal?" their unexpected guest replied. "Aren't you going to introduce me?"

Lianna jumped in before Roland could protest the introduction. "Arin, this is Harris Wilson, Sub-Commander."

"My Second," Roland said, "For now." he added, making sure his displeasure was as obvious as possible.

All of four of them stood around the table, hesitant to be the first to move. "Well, don't all stand on my account," Harris said as he pulled out a chair, happily breaking the tension. A brief interval of silence passed as they each took their seats and served themselves. No one was willing to be the first to take a bite.

"And what, pray tell, made you extend our invitation, Lianna?"

Roland asked. He assumed it was better to let her plans unfold than attempt to fight them.

"I thought Harris could explain the nanite removal procedure to Arin," she explained casually. Roland's eyes darted in Harris's direction, freezing him midway through his first bite.

"Are you a nanospecialist?" Arin asked, drawing Roland's burning gaze back toward him.

"Not exactly," Harris responded as he chewed.

"A doctor then?"

"Of sorts."

"Harris has charge of all our medical operations here," Roland explained, wanting more than anything else for this conversation to come to whatever conclusion Lianna had been planning for. "He works very closely with our doctor, who is a specialist."

"Explain away, then," Arin said. "I'd like to hear how you can manage what some of the best minds in the world have deemed impossible."

Roland gripped the arm of his chair, actively fighting the urge to punch his cocky prisoner right in the nose. Lianna traced her fingers over the back of his hand, relaxing his tension.

"Our doctor has developed a…"—Harris tore his bread into several tiny pieces as he searched for the right word—"a substance, which will fight a war against the nanites."

"A war?" Arin questioned with an obvious degree of doubt. Roland's hand tensed up again.

"It's designed to kill anything inorganic in your system," Harris continued. "They can't fight it because it won't harm you. They're not programmed to oppose it."

"It's safe," Lianna interjected.

"Theoretically," Harris corrected.

"So, you've never tried it before," Arin said, with some doubt starting to enter his voice.

"You present us with a unique opportunity," Harris said with a devilish smile on his face.

Arin's eyes scanned the table as he considered. Anything he might be feeling remained inscrutable, but his mind was obviously running through every scenario he could imagine. "What happens if I refuse?" he asked.

All eyes at the table turned toward Roland. Finally included in the conversation, he thought, and was able to completely relax his hand. "I can't let you out into the world. You have a signal attached to your body, and you've been inside the stronghold of what remains a completely clandestine Resistance Army, protecting a treasure entirely unknown to the Unity. Information about who we are, and where we are, would be enough to buy your life back. Maybe even your command."

"I have no desire to get my position in the Unity back," Arin responded without any hesitation or doubt. "I wouldn't have followed Lia here if I did." Roland found the sudden humility in his voice unnerving.

"Nonetheless," Roland said, "you can't expect me to trust you implicitly." Roland prepared himself for more argument, debate, and even more insolence to come from Arin, but the next person to speak was Lianna.

"I do."

**THE WORDS HAD** left Lia's mouth on instinct. It was true but not the kind of truth she wanted to say in front of Roland. She watched his hand take another white knuckled grip on the arm of his chair and knew she had to say something else, something that would erase whatever he was writing in his mind. She slipped her fingers between his, looked into his eyes, and asked, "Would you keep him in the cage indefinitely? Give him years to build up knowledge about us, along with enough resentment to use it?"

He kept his eyes fixed on Lia. "Probably not." Roland was not one to hide his intentions.

Lia flicked a glance at Arin, certain that her pledge of trust in him would have earned her one in return or—at the very least—that Roland's overt threat would have stirred some emotion within him. He showed none. Her eyes must have lingered too long because she soon felt Roland's burning into the side of her face as he siphoned a tense breath in through his nostrils. Lia looked back down at the table for fear that, even without speaking, she had already admitted to more truths she didn't want shared with Roland. She listened to the oppressive silence of indecision coming from Arin's side of the table, the creak of Roland's chair as he leaned harder against the arm. Harris was the only one who continued to eat.

"Then I want them removed," Arin said, breaking the silence.

That same sense of elation raced into Lia. There was a chance now, to keep Arin safe, to restore him back to humanity. She hadn't realized how much it was what she had wanted all along, until that very moment. She felt like laughing out loud but was swiftly reminded not to let any of her joy surface, as Roland's had tensed up again, squeezing her fingertips.

"You would give up immortality?" Roland asked, as if daring Arin to change his mind.

"Seems I will be either way," Arin responded, showing no fear, no resentment, no emotion at all. He turned toward Harris, catching him mid-bite. "How soon can you do it?"

**LIA COULD FEEL** the guard marching up behind them, inching too close for her liking. She glared at him over her shoulder. He immediately slowed down, giving her and Arin enough space to continue their conversation, though Arin did not seem very shy.

"You handed my life to them," he said, without any regard for his volume.

"I gave you the chance to walk away," she said in a harsh whisper. "You and I both know that if you had, you'd be dead by now." She hadn't let the thought sink in before, but it was the most likely outcome if she had left him in the desert. Saying it out loud now chilled her to the bone. "Now, you can walk out of here with your life, your humanity, and your freedom. That's more than you've ever had since the day you signed it all over to the Unity." She was convincing herself as much as she was him.

"If I walk out of here at all," he countered.

"They saved my life, Arin. Simply because they could. Does that make them sound like the kind of men who plan to dismember you?"

"I present them with a unique opportunity. You heard it. This is an experiment. I'm nothing but a lab rat."

Lia couldn't think of what to say in response. The cold reality was that he might not survive. She searched her mind, desperate to grasp some positive thought, some words of comfort. That's when she heard the guard's footsteps closing in on them again. Her desperation morphed into anger. She whirled around and snapped, "I said get back!"

Lia led as they descended the last staircase and made the final turn toward the medical lab. The heavy steel door at the end of the long hallway was sealed. There was still time to talk to Arin, to reassure him, and herself, that this was the right decision. She instructed the guard to stay at the foot of the stairs. He nodded and took up position in the middle of the hall, assuring there was no way but forward.

She led Arin a few paces away, then grasped his forearm, slowing him down to a stroll. "You know this is the only chance you have, right?"

"I've weighed up a few other options," he said in a calculated manner, "but I am aware that making myself enemies on both sides of the world would be less than beneficial. At least by choosing this, regardless of the outcome, I won't be stuck in a cage anymore."

"Is that the only reason?" Lia asked, searching Arin's face for some hint of emotion.

"It's the most logical thing to do," he answered, showing none. They strolled on in silence until they reached the door. Lia could see the large bolt twisted into the locked position. She took in a deep breath, raised her arm, and pounded on the door with her fist.

ROLAND KEPT HIS eyes focused on the blue glow of the screen across the room as it gently blinked the words ENTER SUBJECT NAME. Harris was busy pacing as he made his case. "It's not as if I didn't think this through, Roland. I had the exact same worries when Lia came to me."

"You give him that injection, and you give him everything." Roland said without taking his eyes off the screen.

"I know what it will do for him," Harris agreed. "But don't forget what it can do for us." He added an animated counting of his fingertips to his pacing. "Government plans, counsel names, battle strategies, weapons manuals, military maps, privileged secrets. His memory recordings will go back to his first day of officer training. Seven years of Unity intel, all from the brain of one former Elite Guard commander."

Roland could finally see the silver lining. It made him feel terrible for ever having doubted Harris's motives. He should have known that, even when agreeing to Lianna's secretive plans, he would have only ever acted with their interest in mind. "And if the formula doesn't take?" Roland asked.

Harris responded with his devilish smile. "Then he won't be around to bother you much longer." He stepped in close and whispered, "But if it works, then not only do we have his brain on file, we also have solid proof that we can turn one of them into one of us."

Desperate knocks, most likely Lianna's, echoed in from the adjoining room. Harris motioned toward the door. Roland held him back. "As long as you're going to be digging around in his memory, then there's something else I'd like you to search for."

Harris raised his eyebrows, intrigued.

LIA PUT HER ear against the cold metal door but couldn't hear any motion from inside the lab. She raised her arm to knock again, then pulled it back. She turned toward Arin, looked into his eyes, and asked, "Which one of you made this decision?"

"There's only one of me here."

"That's not true. There's the man who would have killed me before he saw my face and the man who chose to follow me across the desert. I want to know which one I'm speaking to right now."

"Would it make a difference?"

"If I have any reason to believe I'm wrong about this, I'll do whatever it takes to protect you, just as you did for me." She scanned his face, searching for any glimmer of emotion. The sheen of his eyes, the straightness of his mouth, firmness of his jaw betrayed nothing. "Please, just give me a sign."

Arin considered for a while and then finally said, "You were right about the food." She only caught the slightest upturn in the corner of his mouth before the deadbolt clacked and the door to the medical lab swung open, but it was enough.

She led him through the door.

# TRANSMUTATION

# TEN

IT WAS AS if he had stepped over the threshold, back into a Unity city. The cavernous room was outfitted as a full surgical lab, filled to the brim with advanced equipment. It shimmered with sterility under the incessant hum of sickly green lights. Arin mused over the irony of how much it reminded him of the room in which he had received his nanite injection. Harris had swept the door open for them with aplomb and appeared to be the only other person in the lab, until Roland emerged from an adjoining room. Arin attempted to peer around him, into the other room, but Roland was quick to seal and lock the door behind him.

"Welcome to the lab," Harris said as she strode in. Arin surveyed the room, making a mental inventory of all the equipment he could identify. A third person emerged from behind a large metallic disk on a jointed arm. He was small and hunched, practically drowning in the lab coat that was a just shade whiter than his hair. "Allow me to introduce you to our specialist," Harris continued, "Doctor Lau."

That's when the hunched figure turned, and Arin could finally see the distinct and memorable face of the infamous doctor he had grown up watching on the vizo. The wide-eyed, ever nervous, Doctor Lau was the inventor of the very nanites swimming through Arin's bloodstream. As far as the Unity knew, he had been missing for over a decade.

The doctor rushed up to shake Arin's hand. He could only stammer in response. "You're... *the* Doctor Lau... the Unity Doctor?"

"The very same," Roland proudly declared from over his shoulder.

"But... you've been missing for—"

"Not missing," Doctor Lau brightly corrected. "Atoning," he concluded in a suddenly serious voice. Arin found himself being pulled into the room by the doctor's small, wrinkled hands as he continued to explain. "Sometimes when you have chosen the wrong path, son, you do whatever you can to find the right one. After all, isn't that why you're here?" His voice was suddenly chipper again.

Arin was still processing the doctor's unexpected appearance when Roland spoke up. "You see, all those great minds that couldn't figure out how to extract your nanites should have simply asked their inventor. Of course, we're the only ones who knew where to find him." Arin could see him smirking with pride from the corner of his eye.

Roland turned toward the door, grasping Lia's hand as he passed. She stood firmly in place. "I want to stay," she declared, her eyes fixed on Arin.

"They need to work without distraction," Roland said.

"I won't move a muscle."

"Then you can do that outside."

Lia gave him an indignant look. A silent standoff, a test of wills, passed between them before Lia said, "Yes, sir." She allowed Roland to lead her to the door. She gave Arin once last glance over her shoulder before the door sealed shut behind them.

In the shock of seeing Doctor Lau, Arin had somehow allowed himself to be sat upon an examination table. He was just starting to come back to his senses when Harris grabbed his wrist. Arin immediately twisted out of his grip and snatched his instead.

"Relax. This isn't a trick," Harris said, yanking his hand back. Arin eyed what was in Harris's other hand, a leather strap meant to hold him down to the table.

"Then why tie me up?"

"We don't know how you'll react. It depends on where the nanites have gathered in the highest numbers. You might experience little pain, or it might feel like your body is on fire. The straps are precautionary just in case you try to rip off your own skin."

"And once they're deactivated?"

"We use an electromagnet to draw them out through your pores. And that part is likely to hurt… a lot." Harris was either taunting him for his own amusement or being entirely honest. On the chance that he was telling the truth, Arin lay back on the table and allowed himself to be strapped down.

Doctor Lau hummed a happy little tune to himself as he attached monitoring nodes to Arin's body. One would think he was about to perform a task as simple as mopping a floor, rather than alter a man's entire body chemistry. Arin felt the need to interrogate rising. "This procedure, this equipment, is it all your invention?"

"Indeed," was all Doctor Lau said in response.

"And the particle pulse gun?"

"Neat trick, isn't it?" he said like an excited child. "Once I increase the range, decrease the weapon size, we will have—"

"A formidable weapon against any Unity soldier," Arin finished the thought for him. Doctor Lau responded by happily tapping his finger to the tip of his nose, then went back to humming as he filled a large vile with a thick, silver liquid. Arin wasn't done asking questions. "Why invent all of this to kill the technology that you perfected?"

Doctor Lau's child-like air suddenly became that of a solemn old man, weighed down by stony regrets. His face fell as he turned to Arin. "Oh no. Perfection is the wrong word, son. Perfection does not exist in you. No, no, no. You are an invention that became a monster, and now, I kill the monster with the invention."

Whether it was Arin's strategic mind, or some hint of fear he might still be capable of feeling, the realization that he had just alienated a man who was about to inject an unknown substance into his living veins filled him with an overwhelming urge to rip free of his bonds and run like the wind. That inner desire must have shown somewhere on the surface because the next thing he felt was Harris's hand on his shoulder.

"Don't worry," he said and then pointed to the doctor. He was back to his happily humming self again, as if a switch had simply been flipped. Arin made note to assure he never flipped it back.

Arin spent another several, mind-numbing, hours staring at yet another ceiling. Harris and Doctor Lau had already shared several secretive conversations in the other room, leaving him alone with the steady blips from his heart monitor. Whatever they had expected to happen was not. Arin had just become certain that nothing would ever change when Doctor Lau somberly announced, "The internal struggle begins."

Arin twisted his head around so he could see the monitor the doctor had been tirelessly watching. Rows of gently undulating lines suddenly jumped into sharp spikes. His muscles began to twitch and tremble, from his fingertips up. Arin tried to control himself, clenching against every pull he felt from every limb, but the tremors soon overtook his entire body.

The pain followed. What began as an electric tingling in his skin became the sensation of a million needles piercing down to his bones. Pain, of any kind, was already a distant memory to him. Pain, in this extreme, was like nothing he had ever felt. Arin clenched his jaw, trying to bear as much as he could, but a surge of sensation overtook him. He cried out in anguish.

Once they had begun, his screams were as uncontrollable as the pain itself. He tried to hold them back with every desperate breath he drew in, but another would soon follow. He barely heard as Doctor Lau called out, "The time has come, Mister Wilson."

Harris jumped into action, positioning the large metallic disk over Arin's writhing body. He primed a switch. A thunderous drone soon overtook Arin's cries of pain. The metallic disk vibrated. The drone grew louder and louder. Just as the pain began to subside, offering Arin a few seconds of relief, the electromagnet reached full charge. He felt every fiber of his being simultaneously sucked toward the magnet. His veins darkened and raised as if ready to burst through his skin. His body felt as if it were being torn to shreds. He emitted one final scream. Everything went black.

Arin had no way of knowing how long he had spent in the black before sight and sound came rushing back to him. It started with a bright flash and a vibrating crack. Shapes began to form through the blur of white that followed. The figures of Harris and Doctor Lau hurried in and out of view. As sound cascaded into his ears, it shaped into voices in panic and the clacking of instruments. He only had a moment to think, *something must have gone wrong,* before it all began to slip away.

As the black slid in again, another crack brought the world back, along with a sudden jolt in the very core of his body. The sights and sounds were clearer now. The figures were no longer rushing, their voices calming to murmurs. Arin felt a sudden warmth radiate from his chest and trickle into every limb, bringing all sensation tingling along with it. The acidic smell of electricity hung in the air.

Arin thought to ask what had just happened but didn't have the chance before consciousness slipped away from him.

**LIA WAS CRUMPLED** against the door. The shock of Arin's last scream had taken her knees out from under her. She pressed her ear hard against the metal, waiting desperately for some sound, any sound, that would tell her he was still alive. The tears she hadn't even realized she had shed were dried to crust by the time she heard something. It was only footsteps, but that was enough. She jumped up and pounded on the door. Harris only cracked the door open wide enough to show his face. "Is he alive?" Lia immediately asked.

"Alive and stable."

She barely gave herself time to draw in breath. "Can I come in?"

"You already know that answer, Lia."

"If you're finished, then there's nothing for me to distract you from."

"He's only conscious for a few minutes at a time."

"That doesn't matter to me." Lia knew that being a nuisance was the best chance she had at getting past Harris.

"I have my orders."

"Ax your orders!" She was preparing to push him out of the way if she had to.

"Easy for you to say. You always get away with violating your orders."

"And Roland never finds out when you violate yours," she said as she raised a knowing eyebrow. If nuisance wasn't going to work, then a thinly veiled threat certainly would. Harris opened his mouth to argue more, then clamped it shut and stepped aside.

Lia rushed to Arin's side and clasped his hand. His skin was pale and clammy. Sweat was soaked through his hair. He turned his head slowly, cracked open bloodshot eyes. He tried to speak, but the words stuck in his throat.

"He needs some—" Harris appeared with a cup of water before Lia said the word. She swept it out of his hands and held the cup to Arin's lips. He could only take a tiny sip, but it seemed to restore him enough for the time being. He glanced from Lia's hand clasped around his, up to her face, silently asking if it was something she should be doing. She gave him a smile, silently responding that it didn't matter whether or not it was. She would do what she chose.

Doctor Lau emerged from the other room, humming his regular tune. As he looked up and saw Lia, his hum morphed into a loud clearing of his throat, directed at Harris.

"You try telling her to leave," Harris responded as he backed his way toward the door.

"I'm not going anywhere so don't bother," Lia said without taking her eyes off Arin.

"See what I mean?" That was the last thought Harris offered before he exited, sealing the heavy door behind him.

Doctor Lau simply tossed up his hands and went about checking the monitors. Arin twisted his head around. "How long will I be like this?" He sounded as if his throat had nearly been torn right out of his body. It made Lia squeeze his hand even harder.

"In your case, son, quite a while," the doctor responded, very matter of fact. "The decimation of such a ripe nanite population, which, no doubt, grew strength over many years of adjustment to your particular anatomical needs, appears to have reverted your body to a state, perhaps even weaker than pre-injection."

"Weak" was all Arin could get out before the words stuck in what was left of his throat.

"As a hatchling!" Doctor Lau said with a manic energy. Then he shuffled off and disappeared back into the other room.

Lia didn't have to guess what Arin was thinking. Doctor Lau's brilliance was equal only to his obliviousness. He had used the last word Arin ever wanted to hear again, weak. She knew it would awaken in him the same rash determination that had made him become a Unity soldier in the first place. How it would manifest itself now, she didn't know.

She felt his fingers twitch. He was already attempting to ball his hands up into fists, his muscles trembling. She distracted him from what would inevitably become a fit of frustration by giving him another sip of water. "You'll recover much faster than he thinks," she assured him. "I did. The doc never accounts for stubborn, willful asses like us."

He smiled, reassuring her that his mind wasn't entirely occupied by Doctor Lau's words. Then he said, "I'm sorry you ever had to go through that."

It was the last thing Lia expected. He was the one lying on the examination table. He was the one who had been nearly torn apart by pain. He was the one facing a long road to recovery, a forever altered mind and body, but his thoughts were of her. She was so taken aback that the only words she could muster in response were, "It wasn't your fault."

"You said yourself, if the uniform fits." Somewhere, deep within those words, he was apologizing for ever having left her.

"Well, you're no longer in that uniform." Somewhere, deep within those words, she was forgiving him.

Color was returning to Arin's face. He lifted one trembling hand and put it gently against Lia's cheek. She placed her hand over his, stilling his tremors. They remained still and silent, savoring the sensation of each other's touch. For a moment, they were both looking through a window into the past that could have been. Then, the reality of who she was now and where she was now hit Lia like an electric shock. She pulled back, gently placed Arin's hand down on the table, and attempted to erase the moment. "See, you're getting stronger already."

She turned away under the guise of getting him more water. "The doc will want you to stay here for a while, but he's pretty easy to convin…." Her words trailed out as she turned to see that Arin had slipped back into unconsciousness. She took a furtive glance at the door to the other room, leaned down, kissed his forehead, and whispered, "It's good to have you back."

**EVEN THROUGH THE** waves of pain and surges of unconsciousness, Arin knew it was Lia's lips that had just touched on his forehead. He had never forgotten what they felt like.

**LIA'S DRESS SWISHED** back and forth as she skipped down the street. Why did she have to go so fast? Arin hated running unless he had to. He chose a speedy walk, with an occasional trot, to keep up with her. She threw a glance over her shoulder at him and laughed. Was she laughing at how he walked or laughing about some other plan she had up her sleeve?

They were nearing the front gate of her house. Arin looked up to see if Mayor McMillan's big red face was watching them through any of the windows, but they all remained empty. He looked back to the sidewalk just in time to see Lia's foot disappearing into the bushes that overflowed through the fence. She was crawling through that natural tunnel that led to the hole under the fence. Neither of them had used it for a long time, so he wondered what had compelled her to choose such an effortful entrance on this occasion. Her arm poked out and beckoned him forward. Obviously, he was meant to follow. He peered into the tunnel between the branches, watched Lia squeeze under the iron bars that had rusted away their connection to the ground, then jump to her feet and race off into her own yard.

He crawled through with measured caution, assuring he didn't scratch himself on a stray branch or a sharp, rusted edge. Lia was doing spins on the lawn on the other side. "Why did you sneak into your own yard?" Arin asked as he approached.

"If we went through the house, Papa would know you were here. He'd keep an eye on us. This way, we have the yard all to ourselves." It was a giggle worthy plan that she had up her sleeve after all. Eventually, she was too dizzy to stay on her feet. She flopped onto her back on a soft rise in the grass and swept her arms up and down, making imprints of wings in the long grass on either side of her body. "Don't you want to join me?"

"On the grass?"

"It doesn't bite."

"I just don't like how it feels."

"Okay." She hopped up without a second thought and raced toward the old tree. Arin trotted along behind her. She began to climb the thick gnarled branches. "You can sit up here with me."

"Aren't you afraid you're going to fall?" She took another wide step up and then looked down at him. He hoped the flush he felt rise up in his cheeks wouldn't give away the fact that he could see up her dress. She probably knew he could and didn't care.

"No." She kept climbing.

He tested his first foothold, firm enough, and climbed up after her. She slid herself out onto a wide branch and then dangled her legs over the edge. Arin settled into the same spot but refused to release the firm straddle he had over the branch. It assured he wouldn't fall unless the branch broke out from under them. "What are we doing up here?"

"Looking at the view. See?" She swept her hand across a break in the branches. It framed a view of the few roofs and spires that poked out above the trees of Waterford. "I like the way the town looks from up here. Like it's mostly trees."

Arin gave the view a token glance, then turned his eyes back down. There was a bloody scrape on Lia's knee. "You're hurt."

"Stupid dresses. I can't do anything in them without getting beat up."

"Here." Arin pulled out his handkerchief and dabbed the dribble of blood away. It looked like it wasn't going to stop oozing, so he held the handkerchief firm against her knee. He looked up to see her smiling at him. He felt compelled to keep talking. "You'll want to clean it so you don't get an infection." That was the extent of the medical knowledge he had learned from his mother's treatment of his many mishaps.

"Okay." She was still smiling. "You know Papa always kisses my scrapes to make them better."

"That doesn't actually do anything."

"It makes me feel better. That's something." She looked back at the view. "You could try."

Arin suddenly felt frozen on the spot but still managed to utter, "Okay." With a few jerky stops along the way, he leaned down and lightly pecked her kneecap. Her skin smelled fresh, like the grass. He looked up to see her smiling at him again. "Did it work?"

"A little." She blushed. "You could try it on the lips, too, if you want."

"Okay," he heard himself say. He scooted closer to her and leaned forward. She leaned toward him. He extended trembling lips to hers. She turned hers up to meet his. Her lips were soft. The light touch of them didn't feel like quite enough, so he leaned farther forward. He heard her take a breath in, then he felt the heat of its release on his skin. They parted slowly, the slight bit of moisture between their mouths causing a momentary tug on each other's lips before they separated.

His heart was pounding so hard he was certain she could hear it. She smiled at him. There was a naughty sparkle in her eyes. For a moment, it looked as if she was going to lean in for another kiss, something he would have gladly welcomed, but then she dropped out of sight.

"Lia!" Arin shouted as she sailed to the ground. His already palpitating heart leapt up into his throat. She landed with a solid thump and fell forward onto her hands. She pushed herself to standing and looked up at him, with dirt on her palms and a cheeky smile on her face.

"That was fun! You should try it."

"No way!" His voice cracked.

"It didn't hurt one bit."

"You're crazy!"

"Then why did you kiss me?"

His adrenaline instantly rushed all the blood into his cheeks. "Because I wanted to." There was no way he could deny that.

"Do you want to do it again?"

"Yes." He didn't even have to think about that answer.

"Then jump!" He considered the height, the potential softness of the ground, the best position to land in. What was the point of all that? He wanted to kiss her again. She'd never let him do it if he didn't jump. "Don't think, just go!" Lia shouted, as if she could hear his brain.

Arin threw legs over the side of the branch, side scooted out to where she had been sitting, took in a deep breath, and shoved himself off the branch.

It was most exhilarating leap of his life.

**ROLAND SWIVELED HIS** gaze toward the doors leading into the grand hall, wary that Lianna might appear through them at any moment. Instead of continuing to protest with his words, Harris was just gripping the balcony railing with both hands, staring out over the horizon as his thoughts processed. Roland knew what he was asking was difficult to achieve, even harder to achieve in secret, but if anyone was a master at tricky tasks, it was Harris.

"Aren't they all intact?" Roland asked. The silence had lasted too long for his comfort.

"Yes, but...."

"Then we should be able to extract every recording. Just as you said."

Harris whirled around to face him. "Recordings of information, facts, knowledge, experiences, yes. But from before injection? Even the doc has never tried that."

"Nonetheless, if a memory has been recalled, it has been recorded."

"If! If it's been recalled! If could also lead to nothing."

"I have faith that the doctor will find something. We will soon know who this man really is. One way or another."

"So, you admit, there are other ways."

Harris must have assumed he was being unnecessarily burdened with an issue of marital trust. Now he was the one failing to see that Roland had their best interests in mind. "None that won't raise suspicion. We can't risk him attempting to escape, not now, and especially not if Lianna felt inclined to help him. The safer they both believe he is here, the safer we remain."

Harris took another moment to think. Roland could tell he was not only resigning himself to the task but taking it on board as a personal challenge. "So, what do we do with our guest in the meantime?" he asked.

"Keep a very close eye on him. And for that, I have faith in you." Roland felt no guilt about burdening Harris with this additional task. If there was anything he was better at than achieving tricky tasks, it was being a masterful spy.

# ELEVEN

**ARIN NEVER KNEW** he could enjoy the simple act of walking so much. Whether he was more grateful that the capability had returned to his legs or that he was able to finally leave the isolation of the medical lab, he wasn't sure. It didn't matter. He was going to savor the sensation of his muscles pushing up every step of that endless staircase.

Lia had talked throughout the day. She told him how the grand building had once been a seat of power for a long-lost leader, then preserved as a museum before it was ransacked by the Unity and abandoned to the elements. She spoke with enthusiasm as she told him how Roland and Harris had found it in this lush valley and restored it as a fortress, giving the locals the sanctity they needed to build up the beautiful city that Cambria had become. Though, she admitted, that had all happened long before she was ever here.

Arin had to keep asking questions about her life, and how it came to be a part of this world, before she would volunteer any details. It was only after they had walked the entire circuit of the balcony and were back inside, wandering the endless halls, that she began to tell her story. She told him about waking up in the medical lab with no notion of how she was still alive let alone how she had come to be there. She talked about the moment she had first seen the immense building and the beautiful city that surrounded it. She bristled with pride as she told him about deciding to stay, to join the Resistor's underground forces. Then she spoke, quite cryptically, about the intense training she'd received under Roland's guidance.

It was only when Arin asked how long they had been married that her responses became short and minimal again, but his desire to understand everything about who Lia had become compelled him to push, even in the face of her discomfort. "It can't be easy, taking orders from your own husband, especially when his commands have you risking your life." Arin knew she couldn't help but respond to that with more than a dismissive word or two.

"He was my commander first, and before that, the man who saved my life. I have no reason to question anything he asks of me." That was the longest response she had given him since the topic of Roland had come up.

"Huh." That was shortest response Arin had given all day.

"You don't believe that?"

"It's just not like you. Not to question. Not to push boundaries. The Lia I knew growing up would never have accepted anything at face value."

"I never said that's what I was doing, and aren't you the last person who should be questioning me about following orders?" She was on the verge of shutting down again, but Arin knew he could keep her talking.

"It's because I know exactly what it's like to blindly follow orders that I am asking." Her face softened. Admitting to his own flaws had kept her from cutting him off, so he dared to ask, "What's the difference? Why stop questioning now?"

"Because there's someone in my life I can finally trust." She turned away and walked on, attempting to end it there, but Arin's determination was strengthening as quickly as his body.

"This isn't exactly the life you pictured for yourself when we were children," he said as he followed on her heels.

"This is the life I choose now. And you can choose whatever life you want now, too." She gave him an icy look over her shoulder. "Control your future."

Arin didn't have to search his memory to know his own words were being used against him. Even with the benefit of seven years' emotional suppression provided by the nanites, that last conversation of theirs had never left his thoughts. She marched right past a pair of doors that he knew they had yet to walk through. Arin had been mentally mapping the entire fortress as the day progressed and was determined to explore every step of it. "What's through here?" he asked and then pushed open the doors without waiting for her response.

Arin found himself bathed in the golden light of the afternoon. He had entered a small, cloistered courtyard, which he judged to be at the dead center of the fortress. Lia was quick to catch up with him and reposition herself in the lead as they strolled into the arched arcade surrounding the courtyard. The reason Lia had skipped this part of the tour became obvious as the center of the courtyard came into view. Roland was fencing with a stout but strong looking man. Another older, but tough-as-nails type, was standing by waiting for his chance.

"Those are our field officers, Emmett and Michaels," Lia explained as if she had intended to bring Arin here all along.

"And what, exactly, are they doing?" Arin asked.

"Training," Lia said. Then she went silent as they walked within earshot of them. Lia tried to rush them past, but Arin intentionally slowed so he could observe every detail. The swords they were fencing with had heavy, curved blades with serrated tips, unlike any style he had ever seen. Roland swung his sword with great speed and equal control. The stout man was able to jump out of the way, but before he could bring his sword forward, Roland's was swinging around to meet his again. With one final clash of metal, his sword was on the ground and Roland's was at his throat.

"Better, Emmett," Roland said as he pulled back his sword, "but you'll need more practice before you can be a front-man."

"Too right, Commander," Emmett agreed as he let out a tense breath and happily backed away.

"You're up, Michaels," Roland instructed. The older man took up the fallen sword and swung it around, getting a feel for it.

They had passed them, but Arin was still watching the match over his shoulder. "Aren't swords a little archaic?" He was speaking to Lia but knew he was going to be overheard. She stopped in her tracks, her shoulders suddenly tense.

Roland was all too happy to answer for her again. "Not when your best chance at victory is to pierce your enemies' heart or sever his head." He gestured accordingly with his sword as he explained.

"So, that's what they're designed for," Arin responded, casually, though he could feel his stomach turn at the idea.

"It's messy business," Roland said, as if he knew what Arin was experiencing. "But since none of the Unis are trained in sword fighting, it provides us with another layer of attack, another little surprise." Roland turned back to Michaels, prepared to go on with his lesson.

"I learned," Arin declared. Suddenly, all eyes were on him. He had spoken without thinking again but was sure he would have said it regardless. Then he felt compelled to fill the silence of disbelief that followed. "In my spare time."

"Of which I'm sure there was a great deal, during your years in command over a walled city." Roland said with a smirk. Michaels chuckled. It made Arin want to take up a sword and skewer them both.

Then Emmett chimed in. "Who taught you?" he asked with genuine interest. Michaels shot him a "snap your mouth shut" look, but Arin welcomed the segue it provided.

"I taught myself," he proudly declared. "I'd be happy to show you what I know," he offered, looking at Roland. Then he heard a sudden, sharp intake of breath from over his shoulder. He had almost forgotten that Lia was there.

"Your muscles are still recovering." She tried to conceal her instinctual fear as reasonable doubt. It only made Arin want to prove her wrong.

"Catch," Roland called out as he tossed a sword toward Arin. He barely made the catch and felt his shoulder dip from the sudden weight of the heavy steel. "They seem fine to me," Roland said. He gestured for Arin to join him in the center of the courtyard.

The others stepped aside, giving them a wide birth, but Arin's ears were sharp enough to pick up as Emmett asked Michaels, "Does he realize?"

"Obviously not," Michaels was quick to respond.

"Should we do something?"

"Sure," Michaels said. "Sit back and watch the show."

That was the last Arin heard of their exchange as he stepped into the full sunlight at the center of the courtyard to face Roland and his sword.

**ROLAND STILLED HIS** mind. He knew he was going to have to make a conscious effort to take it easy on Arin. Despite his desire to teach this privileged, pseudo-solider a lesson by severing one of his appendages—nothing he would miss—Roland still believed in good sportsmanship. After all, this former tin can had no way of knowing that Roland had taken up his first sword at the age of eleven, that he had been trained, by the age of twelve, to target every spot on the body that would drain a man dry before he even noticed he was bleeding. Then again, Roland thought, if Lianna had told him this, and one of his limbs should still happen to connect with my blade, it would be his own fault.

Arin swung the blade around, testing its weight. He did his best to conceal that his shoulder muscles shuddered on the upswing, but Roland had gotten very good at pinpointing his opponents' weaknesses. Arin got into position and nodded his readiness. They began to circle each other.

Roland faked the first two swings, pulling back just as Arin defended. Arin tried the same, but Roland was never going to fall for that. He noticed Arin's hand take a tighter grip on the handle and prepared to defend. The first two metallic clangs echoed around the courtyard. Roland had blocked Arin's attempts with no effort. He stepped in for his own. Another two swings and another two blocks. Arin had matched Roland's speed well and had resisted the urge to step back. *Perhaps,* Roland thought, *there is a fighter in this one, after all.*

"What made you want to learn?" Roland asked as took another wide—and very easy to avoid—swing at Arin.

"It was another skill to know, even if a bit outdated," Arin said as he dared to attempt a jab. Roland smashed his attempt off to one side, throwing Arin off balance.

"It's a very useful skill for us." Roland allowed Arin to get back into a proper stance before throwing another swing at him. This time, Arin couldn't help but step one foot back.

"Hand to hand combat can't be that useful against someone who is stronger than you." That was all it took to make Roland forget about going easy on him.

"The first time a Uni came after me, I was ten years old," Roland said as he stepped in close for another swing. "I had never used a gun in my life, and the only weapon I had was this knife." He had ample time to gesture to the hunting knife on his belt before Arin took another two swings. Roland blocked with more energy, forcing Arin to sidestep. "In a panic, I threw it at him. It flew straight into his chest. It took some time for enough blood to pour out of his body that he had nothing left to heal his wounds, but he still died, right where I dropped him with my knife."

Arin stepped into another jab. Roland twisted out of the way with grace, then threw a quick array of sharp swings at Arin, forcing him into a messy defense. A cacophony of clashing of metal followed. Arin was forced back and back but did not relent. They locked swords at each other's chests, holding a firm front against one another. "It was a blade that saved my life that day and has many times since," Roland said as he eyed Arin over their crossed swords.

"Why would a solider come after a ten-year-old kid?" Arin asked, attempting not to show how hard he was struggling against Roland's strength. It's time to bring this to an end, Roland thought, and made one final push that threw Arin to the ground. He tucked his sword under Arin's chin and stopped just short of touching the skin. Arin froze, his eyes fixed on the blade.

"Because after he killed my father, the only thing standing between that soldier, and the thirty parces of farmland he murdered him for, was me."

Arin eyes turned up to meet Roland's. "You were in Willowdowns?"

He had not only put together the facts of Roland's story rather rapidly, he had done so with a sword pointed at his throat. Now Roland was certain it must have been Arin's intelligence that had earned him a command position because it definitely wasn't his physical prowess. Something compelled him to keep the sword poised at his throat as he answered. "I am the sole survivor of Willowdowns."

Suddenly, Roland was looking into the face of a man who was truly saddened by what he had just heard. He had assumed Arin to be as cold and heartless as all his enemies, but here was someone who, no matter what his orders, would have never done the same. Roland quickly reminded himself that whatever empathy Arin was feeling for him now only existed because the doctor had restored it. He might no longer be his enemy, but he had still been one of them.

Roland pulled his sword back and offered Arin a hand up. He had earned at least that much. Once they were eye to eye again, he said, "Finish your recovery. Then we'll see what you can really do." To his surprise, Roland found himself genuinely looking forward to their next match. He gave him a respectful nod as he took back the other sword, then turned away to return to his lesson.

"I want to fight for the Resistance," Arin declared.

Roland, and all his thoughts, came to a dead standstill.

**THERE IT WAS,** the inevitable manifestation of Doctor Lau telling Arin he was weak. Lia had run through every possible outcome in her imagination. This was the one she feared the most, though she also knew it was the most likely. The audible gasps had already cleared the air, and still, Roland said nothing. He hadn't even moved.

Lia felt the pull to intervene. She stepped between them. "You can't be serious," she said to Arin.

"I am." One look in his eyes confirmed that he was.

"You didn't know," Roland said without turning around. "You didn't know who we were, where we were, or even what we were." He finally whirled around and pointed toward Lia with his sword. "You didn't even know she was one of us. And yet, after a few short days within these walls you want to be one of us?"

"There is no us versus them. There is only doing with what is right versus what is wrong," Arin said, unflinching.

Lia was grateful to see Roland lowering his sword, even as he slowly closed the distance between them. "Tell me then, how you came to this decision," Roland invited.

"I didn't join the Unity to fight for the Unity. I wanted to build a better world. It only took a short time living on this side of it to prove that I wasn't. I want to rectify that."

"Then, by all means, find yourself a piece of land and start building."

"I'm no civilian, and I'm certainly not a prisoner. I'm a solider," Arin said, straightening up as tall as he could. Roland went silent again, his eyes fixed on Arin's.

"Arin, you have absolutely no idea what you're getting yourself into," Lia said, breathlessly.

He flicked his eyes her direction. "You're right. I don't." He looked back at Roland. "But I see no better way to find out."

An electrically charged—yet completely silent—exchange was taking place between them. Everyone else remained still, waiting. After a short time, they somehow came to an understanding. "Finish your recovery," Roland reiterated, "then we'll find out what you're willing to fight for." He pointed with his sword toward the door, commanding an end to the discussion.

Arin was the one marching off ahead as they went back into the maze of hallways. "Dammit Arin!" Lia shouted as she caught up to him. "You can't just switch sides for the sake of continuing to be a soldier. Pledging yourself to every fight you encounter is not how to prove your strength."

He grasped her shoulders, assuring he held her attention steadfast. "I wasn't lying when I said I was wrong. My beliefs have changed, because of you."

He reached into his pocket and exchanged something from his

clenched fist into Lia's hand. She looked down to see the fallen stars from his commander's uniform sitting in the center of her palm.

"You can destroy those now, too," he instructed her, then walked off without another word. That's when Lia knew, whether motivated by Doctor Lau's words or not, there would be no changing Arin's mind now.

**LIA FIGURED IF** she waited until dark, Papa would give up on getting the tree chopped down that day. If he hadn't forgotten by tomorrow, she would simply find another way to delay it, again and again, until he gave up entirely. It had worked so many times before, she was sure it would work again. Then she could keep her perch, her escape, her sanctuary.

The brambles on the other side of the fence rustled as Arin hoisted himself to the top. They had both gotten too big for the hole in the fence a long time ago, but since Arin had sprouted up, almost overnight, it was not a struggle for him to simply climb the fence. Papa would inevitably see him in the yard, but Arin still found the climb over the top easier than the interrogation he would get if he tried walk in through the front door.

He spotted the ax lying next to Lia on the lawn. "People don't normally use axes to trim the weeds," he said with a smile as he sat next to her. She wasn't in the mood. "What's wrong?"

"Papa wants to cut down the tree. He says it's old, diseased. That it's just going to take down the other trees when it falls."

"He's right." Arin agreed without hesitation. Lia gave him a hurt look. It hadn't just been her sanctuary but theirs. "Once you chop into it, you'll see. It's hollow. It's got nothing inside to keep it alive." He was trying to reassure her with logic, again. She hated that. Determined to make his point, he grabbed the ax, headed to the base of the tree, and raised to strike.

Before Lia could protest, her father's voice boomed across the yard. "Timothy! Put that ax down before you hurt yourself." He had his head poked out of the window that he had, doubtlessly, been watching them through. Arin tossed the ax aside. "Lianna, go get the Chambers boy like I asked you to. He'll take care of that old tree for me." Whether reassured that Lia was about to do his bidding, or that he had, at least, paused a potential make-out session, he ducked back inside and closed the window.

Lia stood with a sigh. Delaying would not work this time, so she faced the inevitable. The next thing she knew, Arin was reaching for the ax again. "What are you doing?" she asked, though she already knew what he was about to do.

He wildly swung the ax with all his might. The blade cracked into the bark and immediately stuck. Arin tried to yank it back out, struggling against the weight of the blade. He put his foot against the tree and finally pulled it out with a jerk. The momentum sent him stumbling back.

"Are you satisfied now?" Lia asked, but his heaving shoulders, the burning look in his eyes, made it clear he was not.

Arin marched back to the tree, lifted the ax over his head, and brought it crashing down against the trunk. Every whoosh of air was immediately followed by a loud crack, as if the bones of the tree were shattering with every impact. Arin's face went beet red as he swung the ax, again and again, putting one gash after another into the ancient gray bark. Lia stood silently by his side, explosions of bark flying up around her, as she helplessly watched the destruction.

By nightfall, the tree was no longer standing.

**CORWIN STARED INTENSELY** at the blackened ruins of the city below. It certainly didn't look like it was full of rabid, flesh-eating, former humans. He wondered why the Unity had never ordered the Guard to take back any of the Scav cities. Even if they were more than just ghost stories, taking them out couldn't be much harder than eliminating a pack of rabid dogs. He briefly considered taking his own Guard into the city, just so he could march back and tell the counsel they had yet another outpost, thanks to him. Then he remembered that his sub-commander was standing to one side, patiently awaiting his verdict.

"Are you sure that plow pusher wasn't feeding you a story?" Corwin asked her without breaking his gaze.

"That's what I thought at first, but he was still saying the same thing even after I... pushed. No one ever goes near it, let alone *in*to it."

"Like scared little rodents," Corwin muttered to himself. He surveyed the lands around the ruined city, a dense and tangled forest, thick with greenery. Traversing that alone was going to take more time than he wanted to spend in pursuit. Securing another outpost would have to wait until after he had that traitor locked in a box. He'd certainly consider doing it on the way back. "Then we go around it," he declared.

"Commander, the transport won't make it through those trees." His sub-commander had never expressed doubt before. He did not appreciate hearing it now.

"Then we walk," Corwin ordered.

"Sir?"

"We walk." It was the last thing Corwin said before marching downhill toward the forested valley. His sub-commander remained to relay the order. The sun was setting by the time the last in the long line of soldiers made it over the crest of the hill and dropped into the forest.

They were getting closer.

# TWELVE

**HE CAUGHT LIANNA** staring out the window again. None of the food or drink, none of the jovial conversation or even crude jokes had brought her entirely into the room that night. As Roland, Harris, Emmett, and Michaels enjoyed their bounty, Lianna drifted between the luxury of their present and a memory of something long past. At times like these, Roland would be given a glimpse into the more sheltered recesses of her mind. When she stepped away from the laughter in the grand hall, out onto the balcony, he chose to follow, with the hope that this might be one of those occasions.

She acknowledged him with a smile, then went back to drifting. Roland decided not to hold back any longer. "If you have your doubts about him, you need only to express them. It's your opinion I trust above all others."

"I don't."

"Then what is it that's playing on your mind?"

The words were there, but she hesitated to share them. Roland ran his hand along her arm inviting a moment of calm, helping her thoughts to release. "When we were children," she finally said, "he wanted to be a scientist or a doctor. Soldier was meant to be a steppingstone. And now, he's been given another chance but—"

"It's all he knows." It may have only been a few days, but that had become obvious to Roland.

"It doesn't have to be."

"Would you say the same about yourself?"

She finally turned toward him. "What do you mean?"

He stepped between her and the view she had been gazing at. "When I looked into your eyes for the first time, I saw the fight in you. It's what helped you to survive then, and it's what has kept you alive ever since. It may not have been the path you would have chosen, but you certainly embraced it once the path chose you."

"Are you saying he's the same?"

"Hardly. That shiny tin can has never had to fight anything more than a staged battle in his entire life." She turned her eyes away. Roland would have to put aside any insults in order to hold her attention. He traced his finger along her cheek, drawing her eyes back. "But I can tell that he wants to. The question is, what has he really chosen to fight for?"

He was asking Lianna, certain she knew the answer, but instead of sharing her thoughts, she simply asked, "Do you intend to find out?"

"I do." She knew very well what that meant for Arin. Roland had a fine-tuned way of testing people, pushing their physical limits until their mental ones revealed themselves. It made for very strong soldiers and very few secrets.

Lianna mulled it over, brooding at first. Then her face changed as the spark of an idea lifted her thoughts. "Then let me help."

"How?" Roland made no attempt to hide the suspicion in his voice. "I'll think of a way."

She had a smile on her face and the sparkle of secretive thoughts in her eyes. It made Roland incredibly uneasy, but as was so often the case when it came to Lianna, he found himself saying, "Fine."

**DOCTOR LAU STOOD** silhouetted against the grand window, hunched over his pocket watch. Arin's whacks against the wooden training dummy echoed around the double storey room. Each hit, jarring at first, was becoming easier to take as Arin's muscles built up a defensive blood flow. His skin was bright red, and sweat had beaded up on his brow by the time the doctor called out for him to stop. Arin breathed intensely up into the air as Doctor Lau attached a node to his chest. The doctor focused on the readouts on a small, boxy portable. "And how are we feeling today, Mister Arin?"

"Fine. Perfect."

"Yes. Yes, I can tell. You're sweating. Your heart's racing." Lau turned his wild eyes up from the portable screen. They grew wide with excitement. "You see, son. I've killed the monster." Suddenly, Arin wanted nothing more than to be detached from the doctor. His wish was granted as the broad doors on the other side of the room were flung open, and Lia marched in, determination in her step and mischief in her eyes.

"He's all yours, Miss McMillan," Doctor Lau announced as he yanked the wire from Arin's chest and shuffled out of the room.

Arin waited until Doctor Lau had closed the doors behind him. "All yours for what?"

"A little test—*if* you're up for it."

"What kind of test?"

"One that will determine if you're really ready to fight without your own built-in hospital."

"I meant what I said."

"We'll see." Lia began to stretch out, cracking each of her joints, jumping around to loosen her muscles.

"What exactly are we going to do here?" Arin asked.

"It's very simple. You fight me. I fight back. Give me everything you've got. I'll do the same."

"I'm not going to fight you."

Lia rolled her eyes as if she knew he was going to say that. "Well, Roland's preference was to use one of the other soldiers. The guard you shot was, not surprisingly, the first to volunteer. But I convinced them that I'd present a sufficient challenge."

"I'm not going to fight you, Lia, because I don't want to hurt you." He could tell that comment had lit a fire in her. It gave him a strong urge to poke at the embers.

"I seemed to give you enough trouble when you were still fully intact," she said, one eyebrow raised.

"I seem to recall shooting you," he responded, poking.

She looked at the nearly healed wound on her arm. "Looks like you missed."

"I'm a fully trained soldier."

"So am I."

His feelings danced between the desire to see what she intended to do and to stir her up a bit more first. He decided on the former. "Fine. Show me what you've got."

They each settled into a fighting stance, cheeky smiles betraying their otherwise hard exteriors. A moment's pause, then they stepped toward each other and began.

Lia jabbed her fists at Arin and sent a kick flying into the air. Each attempt sailed past him as he leaned away. "Don't just mess with me. Do something," she demanded.

"Okay." Arin obliged by throwing several punches at her, but Lia danced away and avoided being touched.

"Now you're messing with me," he said.

"Maybe I'm just faster." That comment lit the fire inside of Arin. He came at her as fast as he could. She blocked one punch after another, sending his arms flying off to the side, until he felt his right fist make firm contact with her jaw.

He instinctively pulled back, instantly afraid that he might have hurt her, but she only used his hesitation to throw a solid punch into his core. Arin felt the wind knocked out of him and found himself stumbling backwards. As soon as he saw her foot closing in to finish him, he knew what to do. He grabbed, twisted, and pulled her to the ground.

She landed with a solid thud but wasn't thrown off her game. She shoved her other foot up into his stomach. The gut busting impact was immediately followed by the sensation of tumbling through the air. His shoulder joints crunched together on impact, but the ping of pain only motivated him to get up faster. He sprung up and spun around, ready for more. She did the same. They launched at each other and locked into a struggle.

"You're hesitating," she said through barred teeth. "That always gives your enemy the advantage."

"You're holding back, too. I can tell." Part of him was hoping she would make this as hard as possible. He was relishing the challenge.

"Fine," she said, "I'll stop." She locked her leg under his. As he felt himself lose balance, he grappled on tight to Lia and brought her down with him.

She dug a sharp elbow into his neck. As the air stuck in his throat, his adrenaline surged. He threw her as hard as he could.

She rolled across the mats and scrambled up again in an instant. He jumped up to face her. They were both flushed, panting, shaking with adrenaline. Perhaps it was more than his body could take yet. Perhaps he was simply enjoying himself a bit too much, but as he launched at her for his next attack, she blindsided him with a solid-fisted punch to his jaw.

It wasn't until he landed on the mats that he realized the sudden strange taste in his mouth was his own blood. It wasn't until he coughed it out onto the canvas that he realized she had robbed him of two of his own teeth. There they lay in the middle of the sticky red pool. Arin felt into his own mouth, almost certain that it was an illusion, but the sharp sting he felt from the gooey holes where they had once been brought visceral reality to the moment. He had actually been damaged.

Lia backed away. "Tell me how you feel now. Now that you can get hurt this easily. That you can feel pain that won't go away within seconds or maybe even a lifetime. Tell me how you feel knowing that every injury will leave a scar."

How did he feel, he wondered. Arin took stock of every sensation he was experiencing. The thumping of his own heart, the air being forced in and out of his lungs, the sweat dripping from his forehead all grounded him in the world. The taste of his own blood was motivating. The sharp pain in his jaw was exhilarating. At that moment, every surge of emotion, every pain, every discomfort made him feel grateful to be alive.

"There are no second chances on this side," Lia continued. "Are you really ready for that?" Arin knew how to answer her. He got to his feet, wiped the blood from his face, and looked at her with a fire in his eyes. She smiled back at him, her fire matching his.

They fought on.

They matched each other, hit for hit. Sometimes it was a contest of speed, sometimes of strength, but the challenges they presented to each other required no introduction. They knew exactly how the other was testing them, pushing them. Neither of them would give in to pain.

Eventually, bruised and bloodied, they were stumbling more than walking as they circled each other. "Go on. You can admit defeat," Lia invited. "I won't make fun of you... too much."

"I haven't lost a competition to you in my entire life." Arin had to suck in another breath. "It won't happen now."

Lia raised her leg into a kick. Arin raised his arm to block. They both lost balance and fell to the mats without touching each other. They lay completely still except for chests desperately heaving in oxygen. Then, they began to laugh. What started as bemused giggles grew louder and more manic, until they were both laughing like lunatics. Soon the laughter mixed with groans of pain and slowly subsided from sheer exhaustion.

Arin rolled onto his elbows and crawled over to Lia's side. She smiled up at him. "You look better with less teeth. Not quite so neat."

He tongued the space where they had once been. "I'm really going to miss those."

"Relax, mister perfect. The doctor can fix that, too." She reached up to wipe a trickle of sweat from his forehead. Then she froze, her hand on the side of his face. Was she going to pull it away, play it off as a meaningless gesture, or leave her hand there indefinitely? He took a chance, reached up, and held her hand against his cheek. He held her gaze and ran his thumb gently over the back of her hand.

They might have remained that way forever if they weren't interrupted by the loud clatter of someone rushing down the stairs. They parted just as Harris burst into the room. "Get ready, soldier," he huffed at Arin. "You're moving into the barracks."

**HARRIS DIDN'T WANT** to think about what he would have walked in on if he hadn't made so much noise coming down the stairs. He wanted to think even less about what would have happened if he hadn't been watching Lia and Arin at all. At least his declaration that Arin was immediately moving into the barracks had been accepted without argument. Then again, why had he agreed so quickly? Why had Lia not said one word of protest as she so often did? Harris didn't want to think about it.

Arin had just completed his third check on the solidness of his freshly replaced teeth when they reached the barrack gates. He straightened up and held his chin high as they headed through. Harris didn't know how the others would take Arin's new bruises, nor the fact that they had been inflicted by one of their own sub-commanders, but he assumed that it was better than going in clean and wound-free. That—combined with his overly proud posture—would only make them hate him more.

Harris spoke as he marched along the muddy trails between the tightly packed cabins, forcing Arin to keep pace or miss out on essential information. "Breakfast is at dawn, and training goes until sundown. You'll be assigned to a unit, and you do everything with that unit." As they arrived at an open square between the buildings, a handful of soldiers stopped in the midst of a sparring match. They went silent, all eyes following Arin as he crossed in front of them. Harris paused his instruction long enough for them to pass out of earshot before turning to offer his thoughts. "I can't promise they'll make this easy on you, but this is your chance to act as one of our soldiers if you really want to become one."

"That's what I'm here for," Arin said without hesitation. Harris gave this some doubtful consideration before deciding it was best to lead on in silence.

They reached the rows of bed cabins. Harris had selected the empty one at the dead center, assuming it would put Arin firmly in the middle of all those eyes that were so keen to watch his every move. Let them do a bit of spying. He stepped aside, offering Arin the lead up the three crooked stairs and in through the ramshackle door.

"This is where you sleep," Harris explained as he followed, "which you will only do when we tell you you can." He pointed to an awaiting gun and holster on the bed. "That is your weapon. I expect you to familiarize yourself with it, maintain it, and wear it at all times." Arin hadn't hesitated to scoop up the gun the moment he saw it. He had already checked the chamber and donned the holster before Harris finished his instruction. "Consider it an extension of your new body. Remember, you're not invincible anymore."

"Don't I get a sword?" Arin asked with the hint of a smile.

There was so rarely any humor in the barracks that to hear a joke out of their latest—and by far strangest—arrival threw Harris for a loop. He couldn't help but crack a smile as he shook his head. He gave another once over to the way in which Arin had straightened up even further since donning his gun holster. "Why are you here?"

"I thought I had already answered that question."

"What I mean is, why put yourself through all of this when you could have just walked out the door?"

"Could I have?"

It didn't take a genius to know the answer to that question, but it did take guts to ask it out loud. Harris felt a growing respect for Arin's intrepidness, even if he questioned what motivated it. He wouldn't have to question much longer. Doctor Lau was just days away from having Arin's memory recordings all scanned and categorized. Harris felt a tinge of guilt about his future task of looking into memories that were more than just military, but orders were orders. He started backing his way out of the cabin. "Next meal is at seventeen hundred in the center of the barracks"

"Thank you… sir." Arin forced out the last word. The former commander in him clearly hated having to use it now, but that was another thing he was going to have to get used to. Harris felt compelled to offer one last thought before leaving.

"Good luck."

**ARIN'S FIRST MEAL** in the barracks proved to be just as horrifically processed as the rubbery protein he'd encountered in that small desert village. He had chosen a table at the edge, knowing he would be watched, judged for all of his actions, until the opportunity to prove himself trustworthy to the other soldiers would present itself. Until then, he planned to use isolation as his survival tactic. Unfortunately, the illusion of safety had made him not as aware of his actions as he should have been. The disgusted face he made at the bowl of gray mush in front of him, and the subsequent glance he had given to the towering walls of the fortress in which—he knew—they were eating much more luxuriously, had been seen.

Two fat hands slapped onto the table in front of him. Arin looked up toward their owner, a stony-jawed man about twice his girth. "What's the matter, Uni?" he asked in a raw voice. "Can't eat without a linen napkin and some dinner music?" Arin simply turned his eyes back down and went about eating his mush. Next thing he knew, the fat hands were grasping his collar. "You still have a superiority complex, huh?" the owner of the fat hands said, forcing breath that smelled worse than the mush into Arin's face. "Doctor forget to remove that?"

Arin hadn't played a game of intimidation like this since he was at the academy, but his memories of it were vivid enough. He knew how to keep himself from being pushed to the bottom of the pecking order. He yanked himself free and smoothed down his collar. "If he had the technology to make personality adjustments, I've no doubt he would have improved yours."

It was hard for Arin not to smile when he heard some of the other soldiers laugh at his clever comeback. Determined to still have the last word, the stony-jawed soldier leaned into his face, dosing him with another waft of toxic breath. "You're nothing but an empty shell now. There's nothing you got, brain or body, that I don't."

He took off before Arin could throw another verbal punch at him. Arin made sure to watch him walk away, knowing it was part of the game. It gave another soldier, a young man with a mousy demeanor, enough of an opening to sit at Arin's table without being invited.

"He's just jealous, you know," he blurted out as he sat. "Phillipe's the name." He extended a hand.

"Jealous of what?" Arin asked as he shook.

"Where you came from. How you got here. Shoot, must be something special in you, man. Otherwise, she would have taken you out. But nah, brought you all the way here instead."

"How do you know all that?"

"Shoot! Word of mouth. News travels fast 'round here."

"So I'm starting to realize."

"She's a legend, you know," Phillipe continued as he shoveled mush into his mouth. "Flawless precision, like a machine. Must have taken out hundreds of your kind."

"My kind?" Arin had genuinely never been referred to like that before. As much as it made his blood boil, it also flooded him with guilt. How many times had he referred to the Resistors the same way?

"You know what I mean," Phillipe said casually. "Point is, she never hesitated to pull the trigger before, so it's got everyone wondering, what makes you so shiny?"

Phillipe paused, genuinely expecting an answer. Arin played it off. "Your guess is as good as mine." He had to ask. "Hundreds you say?"

"Believe it or not," Phillipe said. "There's only one better. Well that's obvious, innit? Or he wouldn't be our leader."

"And how do you know that? Word of mouth?"

"Shoot no! I saw it first-hand," he declared excitedly and then leaned in close to tell his story. "Unity tore up my town nearly eight years ago, but the occupation didn't last long. Nobody saw them coming. The commander led 'em in through the shadows. The fight started with a shower of bullets. Next thing you know, only half them Unis were left standing. The rest were torn down when the Resistors swarmed like locusts. Nothing left but a pile of uniforms in a pool of blood. He fought like it was an art. It was obvious then which side of the line I wanted to be standing on."

Arin had heard stories like that before but had been told that that's all they were. Small contingents of Unity soldiers on the fringe had been known to disappear from time to time. His superiors played it off as isolated pockets of Resistance activity which hadn't affected more than those few who could easily be blamed for letting their guard down. Now he knew who was really to blame.

"I've never thought of killing as an art." That was all he could think to say.

"You will," Phillipe said. "But I'm surprised you don't already. She's just as much an artist as he is."

Phillipe went on eating, but Arin had suddenly lost his appetite.

**HARRIS WAITED, STILL** and silent, between the buildings, confident that he was invisible in the patch of darkness. Phillipe strolled by, casually whistling, making a show of it. Harris took one quick glance around to assure no one could see them, then yanked Phillipe into the shadows. "You can quit the act. Just give me your report, soldier."

"Like you thought, sir, he's not too popular 'round here. Can't see why not. He seems all right to me."

"What has he said about the sub-commander?"

"Ain't said much about her, and believe me, I was yammering."

"You don't have to convince me of that."

"He's not said much about anything actually. I could keep him talking though, with the proper motivation."

Harris rolled his eyes and slid the bottle out from under his jacket. Phillipe eyed the golden-brown liquor inside as if it were a stash of jewels. "Don't interrogate," Harris instructed, holding the bottle just out of Phillipe's reach. "Just listen and watch. Tell what he says. Tell what he does. That's it. Keep everything else to yourself. Understood?"

"Yes, sir. You got it, sir." Phillipe said it to the bottle, but that was good enough for Harris. He handed it over to the starry-eyed young-ster and walked off.

Reliable help really was hard to find.

# THIRTEEN

**ARIN WOULDN'T HAVE** slept that night, regardless of how claustrophobic his cabin was. His mind was busy piecing together a puzzle.

Moments were replaying over and over, as if his recordings, though absent, had somehow returned to torment him. The last bullet from Lia's deadly rifle had zipped right past his head. She had spoken so coldly about missing the assistant counsel. She had called him a "top tier target." Roland's anger had betrayed him as soon as Arin told him his rank. *"Especially skilled at taking out Guard commanders and the like."* Roland had said it with the intent of making Arin uncomfortable, but perhaps it was more true than he realized. She had killed hundreds, Phillipe said. The number was doubtlessly exaggerated, but the notion hadn't come from thin air. Lia had more than proven her skills. She had admitted to never questioning orders.

So, the real question was, just how many had Roland ordered her to kill?

Arin heard the distinct crack of a bullet slicing through the air in the distance. He rose from his rickety bed and dared to peer out the door. The rows of boxy cabins showed no sign of the lives inside. The sound hadn't stirred any of the others. Arin poked his head out farther and listened. Another bang echoed over from just beyond the rise of the next hill. After a short pause, another followed. Arin knew this sound from his training days. It was a sniper practicing on long range targets. Following a hunch, he dared to step out of his cabin and sneak away from the barracks.

**THE GRAPEFRUIT EXPLODED,** splashing its rotten innards onto the neighboring fruits. Lia picked her head up from behind her scope and breathed out her frustration. Rotten or not, its flesh hadn't been her target. Even at night, this shouldn't have been so difficult for her. This orchard was her training ground, her home turf where, no matter what the season, she could drop any fruit from the tree without so much as nicking its flesh. She blamed her last failure on her softening focus. The bruises from her fight with Arin were starting to swell up around her eyes. That must be it, she told herself, as she lined up another shot.

The stem of the fruit was hidden in the shadow of the leaves, but the moonlight bouncing off its curved surface told her where to aim. Lia breathed out slow, stilling her body, her heartbeat. She hooked her finger into the trigger and pulled. The grapefruit dropped from the branch and out of her site. She smiled, relieved, finally at ease but only for a moment.

"No wonder they call you a legend." The sound of Arin's voice made Lia instinctively whirl around and take aim in his direction. He slowly emerged from the trees, hands in the air. As his face cleared into the moonlight, she pulled back the rifle.

"What are you doing here?" she asked in a harsh whisper.

"I took a chance that the sniper fire I heard might be coming from your gun."

She glanced around as if she expected someone else to emerge at any moment, then pushed Arin back into the shadows. "You can't be here. You can't leave the barracks without permission."

"I took a chance on that, too. I needed to ask you something." He paused as he considered his next words. Even in the moonlight, Lia could see the red cracks of exhaustion that had invaded his eyes. Whatever was on his mind had made him just as restless as she was. "Was I a target?" She couldn't answer him, but she also couldn't look away. He insisted. "When you came to Caldera, what were your orders?"

"Take them out by rank," she admitted without tearing her eyes away. "Head Counsel, Assistant Counsel, Guard Commander. You were my third target."

Arin nodded as if he had already figured that out and just needed to hear her say it. "And if you had moved just that little bit faster? If I hadn't moved as fast?"

"I didn't know it was you," she whispered.

"Would it have made a difference?"

Suddenly, Lia felt as if she were being interrogated. "How can you ask that?"

"You're the one who said you have no reason to question what he asks of you."

"And you've given up your right to question him now. That was your choice, remember?"

"Same as yours." Arin put his hands up, cutting off the protest she was about raise about him daring to make her choices a part of the conversation. "But what if he puts a gun into each of our hands and tasks us with killing each other?"

"That would never happen," she said with the firm conviction that would have gone into the protest that he cut off.

"How can you be sure?"

"He's *not* a murderer, Arin!" Zeal had overtaken Lia's volume. "Fighting is a means to an end. A way to give this world back to the people who've been forced out of it." She took a moment to reset. "He's not a killer, and neither am I."

"I didn't say you were." Arin was quick to correct, but the damage had already been done.

Lia felt tears threatening to emerge. She sucked them back. "What is this really about?"

Arin finally took the time to consider what to say next rather than launch back into interrogation. "I just wonder, what's going to happen when all of these troops march into the borderlands, take back the cities, the farms. Won't we just be making the Unity this world's second-class citizens? Won't we just be forcing them to the fringe?"

"I wouldn't draw such a comparison if I were you." She was no longer hurt. She was angry. Arin had obviously sought her out to speak his mind and seemed to care very little about the effect his words were having on her.

"It's not any different, is it? Think about it, Lia. He plans to take it all back by force. He controls the army, the hospital, the land. If we stand a chance against the Unity, I mean really stand a chance, how long is it before this army becomes the new government? Before Roland becomes a new king?"

The question had never entered her mind. She could not deny that it had stirred something in her, some feeling of doubt that had never emerged before. Roland had done nothing but build a new world, a better world, for everyone around him, but his desire to take back what had been robbed from him as a child was undeniable. Throwing stumbling blocks into the Unity's path every time they stepped into their world might not always be enough for him. Even so, the audacity of Arin to say that now, after he had committed his very life, the life he owed to the man he was now questioning, burned Lia up inside.

"Well, he's your king now, Arin. Good luck under the new regime." Lia backed away before Arin could get another word in. She didn't want to hear anything more. "Get back to the barracks, soldier," she ordered and then turned away, leaving Arin alone in the darkness.

It had been a long time since she had let Arin's thoughts invade hers. She was not going to let it happen now.

**LIA FELT ARIN** tugging her gently back as they approached the gate. His fear of being seen by her father always set in at about the same place on the sidewalk. She was determined to get him over that, eventually. For the time being, she was happy to accept the goodbye kiss that she knew came next. It was her favorite part of the afternoon. As always, it was soft and gentle and perfectly formed, as if their faces slid together like puzzle pieces.

"I guess this is goodbye… for now," she said.

"For now?" he asked with a crack in his voice and a smile on his face.

She leaned in close to him. "I'll leave the window open."

He sucked in a deep breath. His hand squeezed hers that much tighter. That got him. She sealed her promise by pulling him in for another kiss. It was better than the first, as was the next one and the one after that. Time swiftly got away from them, along with any memory of where they happened to be standing.

*"Lianna!"* Her father's voice exploded into her ear. Arin leapt back like a startled rabbit. He stammered as if he was going to come up with some plausible explanation for what was happening. One scowl from Papa snapped him into instant silence. "You're coming inside right now!" He barked out as he snatched Lia's arm. She squirmed and complained as vocally as she could as he dragged her through the gate, but it accomplished nothing. He slammed the gate, practically pinching off Arin's nose, and marched her into the house.

He didn't stop hustling her through doors until they reached his study. "You can't just go dragging me around like that, Papa!" Lia thought a plea on behalf of her physical well-being might earn her an apology.

"I can do whatever I damn well please, thank you. Now you sit." No apology followed.

"No!"

"You sit down and listen to me right now, Lianna." He mimed for her to shut her mouth and pointed to a chair. The truth was, she wondered why they had come all the way to his study. The only way to find out was to do what he said. That didn't mean she had to act like she wanted to. Lia sat, crossed her arms, stared down at the carpet, and breathed hard through her nostrils.

Papa paced and said nothing. He took his pacing over to the bar, served himself a drink, and still said nothing. Lia breathed harder, hoping it would at least encourage some annoyance. He only paced a moment longer, then sat in the chair opposite hers.

"That boy isn't good enough for you." She looked up at him, genuinely confused. "What? Where you expecting me to tell you to stop seeing him? To stop sneaking out of the house to run around and do, I don't even want to know what, with that boy?"

"Well... yes."

"I've given up trying to tell you what to do. It doesn't get me anywhere." He tried to hide it by taking a sip of his drink, but Lia saw a slight smile sneak across his face. "But I'm hoping that you'll at least listen to what I have to say. I know what I'm talking about."

"You're only saying he's not good enough for me because you never liked him."

"I never liked him for the same reasons that make him not good enough for you," he said with a point of his glass.

"He's the smartest kid in the entire school, probably the whole town."

"Smarts aren't everything. Far from it."

"You're just saying that because it's Arin. If he was the most athletic one, you'd be saying that wasn't everything."

"That boy doesn't even have the pride to go by his given name," he added with another point of his glass in the general direction Arin would have left from, if he left at all.

"So, he hates a decision that was made for him before he was even born. What a crime!"

"Enough!" It was a shout of annoyance rather than anger, but it was still loud enough to rattle the cubes in his glass. "You do derail a train, don't you?"

Lia went back into her silent stupor while her father took a moment to rethink his approach. "Do you know how proud I am of you?" He put his big hand over her clenched-up fist. Her fingers relaxed in the warmth emanating from his palm. "I know I don't go easy on you, but that's because I expect the best out of you, because I know what you're capable of. You're a natural born leader, you know. Twice as smart and twice as confident as I was at your age. I only got this far. I can't even imagine how far you'll go some day, how many people you'll be able to take charge of, to inspire with your energy. I don't want you to lose that."

His eyes were sparkling with the very pride he was telling her about. The warmth traveled up her arms and into her chest. This was far from the admonishment she was expecting, but there was something about this conversation that she just didn't understand. "What does this have to do with Arin?"

"Argh! The one-track mind of a teenager." He threw back the last of his drink to calm his aggravation. "Our world has changed more since the day you were born than it had for centuries before that. And it will only keep changing. The war may be over, but the fighting goes on. People divide up, pick sides. One day, everyone on one side will be the scared, the weak minded, the spiritless followers. On the other side will be the strong, the brave, the fearless leaders. That boy may be smart, brilliant even, but he has a weak spirit. You do not. Don't let blind, thoughtless passion take you to the wrong side."

Lia leaned back in her chair. Her father did the same. It was so much more than she expected him to say. She had to let it sink in. His faith in her was pleasing, even if a little daunting, but his distrust in Arin seemed unfounded. It had to be a father's prejudice obscuring his view. Lia made sure to stow away any hint of attitude that she'd forced into her posture and voice so Papa would know she was serious when she spoke again. "I think you're wrong about him. Even if everything you said comes true, he won't pick the wrong side. I know he won't."

She was pleased to see that talking about Arin hadn't instantly annoyed him that time. He leaned forward and put his hand over hers again. "I hope you're right. Because a brilliant mind in the wrong hands is a dangerous weapon." He gave her hand a light squeeze, then got up and left Lia alone with his words.

**"THEY'RE TOO CLOSE."** It was all that Roland said, but the weight of his words hung in the room like a fog. All eyes were focused on the maps laid out on the table. The red outline indicating the last known location of the Unity troop was a couple of days' hike away from the borders of Cambria.

"You're sure it was the north woods?" Harris asked.

Emmett confirmed with a nod. "Came from the best traveled trader in the region. He knows those woods better than anyone. A full legion, he said, camped out right in the center."

"But where did they come from?" Michaels asked.

"There's only one occupied city close enough," Harris said. "And only one trail that could have led them from there."

All eyes turned toward Lia. She had felt that moment coming since Emmett told them what he had learned, but the accusatory stares now turned her direction made her want to run. Roland approached, slowly, like he was closing in on a wild animal. "Did you leave alive any Uni capable of recognizing you? Anyone who knew that you fled the city with their Guard commander?"

"Not intentionally," she admitted. Harris let out a huff of disappointment. Roland tightened his jaw. Lia kept a brave face. "It was only one soldier who saw me."

"One soldier who has, no doubt, confirmed your identity with every dust dweller he passed. Otherwise, they wouldn't be standing on our doorstep as we speak." Roland pointed into the center of the red outline as he spoke.

"I tried to take him out," Lia stammered in her own defense. "Things didn't go according to plan."

"Tell me about it," Harris said from the other side of the table. Suddenly, Lia felt no qualms about defending herself.

"I suppose you would have succeeded?" she snapped at him.

"I wouldn't have dragged a Uni tag-along back if that's what you mean by success," he snapped back.

"Then why don't you go next time?"

"Enough!" Roland silenced them both. All eyes focused back on him. He leaned on the table, scanning the maps as he formulated his words. "All this does is bring our plans forward." He looked to Harris, who agreed with a nod.

"What plans?" Lia asked, suddenly on edge.

"In a matter of days they will have Cambria in their sites. We have to make sure that never happens and that not a single one of them makes it back to report anything about where they've been or what they've seen."

"That's a large contingent to take out," Michaels said.

"One they're sure to come looking for eventually," Emmett added.

"Exactly," Roland agreed with a nod. "And when they do, we'll be ready to meet them. The next troop the Unis send will never get this far. And the next will make even less ground."

"You're talking about edging into the border territory." The reality came crashing into her mind. "Not an underground movement, not throwing a stumbling block in their path, but starting an all-out *war.*"

"It was inevitable," Roland said.

"It's what we've been preparing our soldiers for all along," Harris added. "It's about time they got a chance to prove their strength." They had talked about this, Lia realized, as she observed the matter of fact way in which Harris affirmed all that Roland said.

"There's still time to take out the one who saw me, the one who led them here." Lia attempted to argue, though she knew it was already too late.

"Yours isn't the only face he knows," Harris said. "Are you going to take out the hundreds of others who remember, very well, what their former Guard commander looks like? It doesn't matter how long you can hide, Lia. He'll never be able to."

It was true. Arin would always be a fugitive, a prize worth hunting down. She knew exactly what it was like to have a price on your head and felt no fear about the fight they faced to stop it, here and now. She was resigning herself to the inevitable when Roland added, "And the man those Unis came this far to find better be prepared to fight for his newfound loyalties. Because I don't think they're here to forgive him."

"He will," Lia affirmed. Even with the seeds of doubt Arin had planted now germinating in her mind, she knew he would fight. When it came to survival, he never backed down.

"Good," Roland said, then took another step toward Lia and leaned in close so he wouldn't be overheard. "Because if his change of heart proves false, I won't be very forgiving either."

Lia felt a sudden chill down her spine. She had witnessed so many other people experience the same thing when Roland spoke to them, but she had, up until now, been immune. Something in Roland's presence, his countenance, had allowed her to see the intent behind his words. There was always a depth of well-being, even in the most imposing of threats. At this moment, the tone of his voice bore with it a depth of unshakable determination. This was a promise. All she could say was, "Yes, sir."

They began their plans to go to war.

ERUPTION

# FOURTEEN

**A FRESH COAT** of light snow covered the ground and muted the colors of autumn's last leaves clinging to the tangled trees. Lia was dressed in gray body armor so she could blend into the stark branches of her treetop hideout. She scanned the clearing below with her scope, covering the same ground over and over just to assure there were no footprints hidden under the fresh layer of snow. The surrounding woods appeared entirely empty.

The tiny orange light flashed from the radio in her ear. Lia was quick to cover it, knowing it was the only thing that might give away her position. Harris's voice cracked through the static. *"Anything yet?"*

"Patience, patience," she said, reiterating it for what must have been the third time. It was, after all, one of her greatest strengths. She could sit in wait for hours before her target came within view. Knowing how much was at stake on this occasion, she would wait for days if that's what it took. Lia hadn't spoken to Arin since their encounter in the orchard. She hadn't even seen him in the rush to ready her snipers for the impending battle. She made a silent wish that he was at least as ready for what lay ahead as she was. Then she resumed her scan of the ground and the surrounding trees.

She would wait as long as it took.

**BEYOND THE CLEARING,** hidden deep among the trees, Arin crouched in hiding with the other soldiers. He sat against the trunk of a wide tree, the cold mud from the ground starting to crack on his cheeks. He was not used to waiting for the battle to come to him. Unity troops were trained to march in as a unified front, buttons polished, guns on display. It never seemed to put them at a disadvantage. Arin had only ever seen people back down when confronted by the wall of dark uniforms closing in around them. Now, as his eyes wandered over his surroundings, only spotting his fellow soldiers when they dared to move, he knew the Unity was hugely disadvantaged. He only hoped it was enough.

He had asked himself many times over how he might feel if faced by one of the guards he used to command. Could he pull the trigger? The more he thought about them, the more their faces came in and out of his mind, the less he came to care. It was as if his sense of responsibility for them had always only been that of a commander, instantly erased with his loss of rank. But there was one face which aroused a deep sense of rage no matter how hard he tried to stifle it. Corwin was responsible for bringing the Guard here. Corwin would have killed Lia and then him. Corwin would do that still if the opportunity presented itself. Arin allowed his rage to build as he sat silently against the tree, knowing that if he saw Corwin's face in the crowd, it would fuel his determination to stop him once and for all.

Arin watched the other soldiers settle into their final positions and then disappear into stillness. He took a deep breath, leaned back, and closed his eyes, becoming invisible against the tree's bark.

**ROLAND SAT IN** wait in the dark frost of the underground dugout. He stared up into the single spot of light filtering down through the camouflaged roof and visualized the moment he would break free into the midst of battle. This was it. The years in wait, the time spent planning, building, repairing all he had found damaged in this world, had led to this moment. The future that had been taken from him was now his to write.

The soldiers behind him were stirring. He turned and brought them to silence with one simple touch of a finger to his lips. He hadn't tried to quell their doubts or worries. It was their fears that would carry them through this battle, that would keep them alive, just as it had done for Roland to this very day. So, he chose, at that moment, to remember everything he had confronted in his life—the pain, the death, all the blood he'd seen spilled on the battlefields before this one. The memories pumped through his veins, filling him with strength. This, he told himself, is where it ends.

He heard Lianna's voice through the radio. *"Hang on,"* she said, *"There's movement in the south."* She sounded calm and ready. Now she'll know what she's truly capable of, Roland thought, as he envisioned the number of Unity troops dropping from her shots alone. He tingled with pride. *"Standby,"* she ordered. He gripped tight to the hilt of his sword and smiled.

Any moment now.

**LIA WATCHED THROUGH** her scope as a glint of light off well-polished metal flashed from between the trees, certain it could have only come from a Unity uniform. "Ready snipers," she ordered through her radio. She snapped her scope onto her rifle, lay long and low across the wide branch of the tree, and steadied her aim. "On my signal." Lia kept a steady watch as the Unity troop emerged into the clearing. Some carried travel packs, others were unburdened, but none of them had their weapons at the ready. She waited and waited as the long line of dark uniforms continued to emerge from the trees, one after the other, until the last one had cleared into view. Then she called her order. "Snipers *go!*"

Shots rained down from the surrounding treetops. Unity soldiers randomly dropped to the ground. Others armed their weapons and scanned their surroundings, but there was nothing to be seen. A moments pause, then another chorus of shots. More soldiers dropped. A voice from below called out, "In the trees!" Those left standing began to fire up into the branches.

Lia flattened against the branch making herself as small as possible. She instructed through the radio. "Push fire. Move them north."

A cascade of shots began from behind the Unity soldiers sending spurts of mud up into the air. Then the shots blanketed across the troops dropping one line after another. Another voice among them shouted, *"Get to cover!"*

Those who were left standing raced into the trees.

**"THEY SCATTERED!" LIA** called through Arin's radio.

Then Harris's voice commanded, *"Second wave go!"*

The Resistance soldiers began to materialize from the surrounding woods, seeming to emerge from the trees themselves. They tore across the underbrush, heading full speed toward the oncoming Unity soldiers. Arin waited with a handful of others until the sounds of fighting drew near. As the smell of gun smoke wafted into his nose, he leapt from hiding and raced into battle.

The surrounding sights and sounds were brutal. The Unity soldiers fired blindly into the crowd mowing down every living thing in their path. The Resistors fought through every injury, clutching at bleeding wounds as they pushed forward. As soon as any Unity soldier fell, he was instantly destroyed by a barrage of bullets. Arin found himself hesitating, frozen in place by the shock of what he saw. Then, the zip of a bullet through the air, the feeling of its heat passing right by his ear, instantly awoke his need to survive.

*Bang! Bang! Bang!*

Three bullets and three takedowns of the oncoming Unity soldiers. Knowing it had to be done, he fired several more bullets into the bodies he dropped. He didn't allow himself to see their faces. It was either them or him. Kill or be killed. He might feel different later, but at least he would still be alive to feel.

Arin pushed further into battle.

**LIA CONTINUED TO** pick off any Unity soldier who dared to race through the clearing below. Spot, follow, shoot. Spot, follow, shoot. It was rhythmic in its simplicity. The pile of bodies was growing, but her confidence betrayed her. She had revealed her position. A bullet cracked through the branches just behind her head. Lia spotted the soldier responsible and took aim, but it was too late.

The next *crack* was followed by instant, white-hot pain as the bullet entered her shoulder. She scrambled around the tree, trying to take cover behind a tangle of branches, but the next onslaught of shots took out the branch underneath her in an explosion of bark. She fell, her rifle clattering into the brambles, her arms grasping at every branch she whipped past in a desperate attempt to slow her descent. Then she felt the hard, cold impact of the frozen ground as it slammed into her back and forced all the oxygen from her lungs.

She was still sucking in breath when the soldier who had spotted her closed in for the kill. Lia rolled painfully onto her bleeding shoulder, whipped another gun from her belt, and took aim at the oncoming Unity soldier. They both fired. Lia heard a bullet *thunk* into the ground behind her at the same instant the Unity soldier dropped. Saved by seconds. Lia stumbled up, fired a kill shot into the soldier's head, and steadied her breathing.

The battle had moved deeper into the trees leaving nothing but a pile of bodies in the clearing. Harris's voice called through her radio. *"Third Wave! Round em up!"*

The battle may have moved, but it was far from finished. She braced against the pain and raced into the trees. Lia zigzagged around the trunks to avoid becoming anyone's target, a gun in each hand. She was skirting the edge of the battle, hesitant to dive into it. There had always been distance between her and her targets. Now, trapped on the ground, the heat of the violence was suffocating. A Unity soldier charged out of the crowd toward her. Combined powers of skill and fear allowed her to drop him with a single shot.

Afraid that remaining still would mean taking another bullet, Lia kept running.

**ARIN FINALLY ALLOWED** himself to see a face in the crowd. Corwin, his uniform shimmering with the fresh blood of countless bullet wounds, appeared between the trees. Arin took aim. Corwin raced straight toward him. As Arin pulled the trigger, Corwin dove at him, taking a bullet to the arm as he threw Arin to the ground.

"I'm taking your body back with me," Corwin said before throwing a punch across Arin's jaw. He slammed Arin's gun hand against the ground, loosening his grip but only for a second. Arin bared his teeth against the struggle, holding tight to his gun, knowing he would need it. Corwin threw another full metal punch into Arin's nose, instantly flooding his face with blood. He threw another at him, causing a momentary flash of blindness. After another, Arin could taste the blood oozing up around his back teeth.

There was a pause in Corwin's onslaught of punches. He was seeing the pain in Arin's face. He was watching the damage get worse without any recovery. It was only a split second, but a flash of satisfaction flickered in Corwin's eyes as he realized they were no longer equals. He gave up on punches and wrapped his hands around Arin's throat. "You're just as pathetic as them now," Corwin sneered. "What happened, soldier? How did they break you?"

As his oxygen depleted, Arin felt a rise of adrenaline overtake him. He concentrated all his energy on his gun hand, shoved it straight into Corwin's chest, and shot. Hot, searing blood splattered across his face. Corwin flew back and hit the ground. Arin jumped up, took aim, but Corwin rolled out of the path of the next bullet. As he stood, Arin's last bullet dropped from his chest. He pulled out his own gun and took aim.

Arin ducked for cover between the trees. He threw his arm around the trunk and took a few wild shots. Corwin reeled back as bullets zipped into his body but then only started coming faster. Speed was the only advantage Arin had left. He took off running. The pounding of determined boots followed close behind. The other fights Arin skirted around didn't seem to matter. This was the only one he had to survive now. A deep-seated instinct told him to keep running.

A heavy weight suddenly slammed into the back of Arin's legs and sent him face first into the frozen turf. Corwin wrapped a vice grip around his legs. Arin kicked and jerked, desperate for freedom, desperate to keep running. Corwin dragged him back. Arin clawed at the ground with his free hand. He snatched a tree root and held on with all the strength his fingers could find. Turn over, he told himself. Just one shot to the temple, and it's over.

Before Arin could twist his body around, Corwin had both knees on back. His ribs screamed out in pain. His lungs struggled to heave against the weight. Corwin pinned his shoulders into the ground and flattened his gun hand deep into the muddy snow. "Look at you," Corwin seethed into his ear. "Finally acting like the coward you've always been."

Those words awoke in Arin something he had never felt before, a desire not only to assure his survival but his superiority. Corwin would not be allowed to inflict pain without feeling it for himself. Arin instantly formulated a plan. He wrapped his fist tight around the tree root and twisted until he felt it crack. Corwin's hands wrapped around his collar. Arin allowed himself to be flipped over, lifted to his feet, and slammed against a tree. Then he shoved the sharp stake of wood straight into Corwin's throat.

QUESTIONS WITHOUT ANSWERS raced through Corwin's mind.

*How did that happen? How did that excuse for a soldier blindside me? How did he get a weapon? What even is this thing? How is he still injured, still bleeding? How did he get his gun? Where is my gun? What is that strange feeling in my gut? Is that blood soaking my chest? Why are my hands numb? Is that my pulse in my ears? What happens now?*

**CORWIN STUMBLED BACK,** choking on his own blood as it poured out around the tree root. This is what he deserves, Arin thought, but as Corwin dropped to his knees, Arin's eyes fixed on the horrific waterfall of blood pouring out of his body. The fact that it could have just as easily been him had he not been the first to deliver a fatal blow provided no comfort. Blood spilled is still blood, and this blood was on his hands.

Arin swore he saw Corwin's eyes bear the signs of true fear as he grasped at the tree root, attempting to yank it out. Arin took aim and fired. Corwin lay still, a smoking bullet wound in the center of his forehead.

Arin felt none the satisfaction he had imagined he would. Seeing Corwin's body on the ground, never to heal, never to rise, never to pursue him again, only filled him with a sense of dread. This was just one man. There would be so many more to follow. This was just the first blood spilled and far from the last.

He backed away and disappeared back into battle.

**THE SOUND OF** engines revving inside the dugout was deafening, the smell of exhaust overpowering, but it was mere seconds before Roland had led the charge crashing up through their cover and out into the woods.

His moment had arrived.

The battle scene was a mess. Soldiers, alive and dead, were scattered throughout the trees. The surprise appearance of the Resistance soldiers on motorcycles had delivered its order, corralling all the battling bodies together like livestock to slaughter. Roland swiftly closed in on the fighting and pulled out his sword.

The action tightened into a single visible tangle in the center of the forest. *Time to end it,* Roland thought as he zoomed toward them. One slash across the throat of a Unity soldier severed his head in a flash of metal. The next he stabbed through the back, hard enough to feel the crunch of the sword penetrating his rib cage and poking through the other side. It was the only way to assure he destroyed his heart to prevent him from healing. The soldier's limp body crumpled to the ground telling Roland he had hit his mark. He rode off in pursuit of another.

Roland plowed through the fight with extreme grace, leaving a trail of blood in his wake. Every impact of his blade felt like progress. Every shower of blood that followed, a victory. His speed increased, and his precision sharpened with every soldier he fell. Roland drove forward with only one thought on his mind, this world will soon be ours.

In the distance, a Unity soldier broke free from the mess of battle and ran for cover. Roland revved up his engine and zoomed after him.

**ARIN AND LIA** both ran into the same clearing and instinctively pulled their guns on each other. Arin pulled his back. Lia's arm remained stiff. A Unity soldier crashed through the trees behind Arin. Lia shot, dropping his body to the ground beside him. She marched up, stood beside him, and shot three more bullets straight into his head.

Once the ringing in his ears had stopped, Arin could hear her breathing, strained, tense. It made tiny clouds in the air. Her hands were shaking. Blood steadily dripped from her fingertips, leaving spots of scarlet in the snow at her feet. She was hurt. She was frightened. So was he.

The sounds of battle were distant now, the immediate threat vanquished. Arin gently put his hand on her shoulder and slid it down her arm, lowering her gun hand. Her breathing slowed. Her muscles stilled. She turned her eyes up to meet his. They shared a moment of understanding, of knowing exactly how one another felt without the need for words.

The sound of an engine roared steadily toward them. Arin and Lia parted as Roland's motorcycle zoomed into the clearing. He rode with his sword forward, his arms and chest stained bright red with fresh blood. Roland cut the engine and left his motorcycle. He approached the body at Arin's feet and prodded it with his sword. His shoulders shook. He was actually laughing.

"That was the last one!" he proudly declared. "We did it."

Lia let out a long, tense breath and turned her eyes away from the body on the ground. Arin's eyes scanned over the blood staining Roland's body, then looked down at the blood on his own hands.

Other Resistance soldiers began to emerge from the trees, weapons drawn and ready. "Success!" Roland shouted out to them. A cheer started to go up all around them, small at first, then it grew and grew, moving in waves throughout the surrounding trees. Arin and Lia looked at each other, remaining still and silent among the din of celebration.

# FIFTEEN

**ARIN SAT ON** his chosen table at the edge of the mess in the center of the barracks. Joining in the fight had only pushed him up the hierarchy enough for the other soldiers to leave him alone. For now, that's all he wanted. The others were gathered around bonfires throughout the barracks, eating, drinking, laughing, and cheering. Discipline had been dismissed for the night. Arin's mind was preoccupied with a question, the answer to which lay out of his reach.

*What happens now?*

He glanced up toward the fortress where sounds of celebration wafted out through the open windows. No doubt, he thought, they're feasting tonight. It wouldn't have mattered if they had offered up some of their bounty to the soldiers below. Arin had no appetite. As he looked up, Lia's distant but distinct figure stepped out onto the balcony, silhouetted against the slit of light from one of the tall windows. He concentrated on her form, trying to catch the subtlest of movements his eyes would allow him to see, so he could glean how she might be feeling.

"Now you know." The sound of Phillipe's voice jolted Arin out of his fixation. "Seen it for yourself, survived to tell the tale, and all that." He pointed up to the fortress. "Like I said, legends."

It took a conscious effort for Arin to pry his eyes away from the balcony and turn toward Phillipe. "You were also on that battlefield. Don't you give yourself any credit?"

"Shoot! Sure I do. But I also know that my green arse would never have lasted this long without them." Phillipe leaned in close enough for his flammable breath to indicate exactly how he'd been celebrating. "And yours wouldn't even be here."

"Can't argue with that."

He leaned back and took another wobbly glance up at the fortress, then back at Arin. "One of these days I'm going to figure out what makes you shiny."

That might have sounded like a threat coming out of anyone else's far more sober mouth, but Arin sensed this was one he could write off. "Let me know when you do."

Phillipe responded with a chuckle that was somehow both knowing and inebriated, then wandered off to celebrate with the other soldiers. Arin bided his time before looking up at the balcony again. He derived an instant calm from the sight of Lia's figure still standing there.

He wondered if she felt the way he did right now.

**LIA STARED OUT** over the vast view, listening to the cheers and laughter below. She glanced at each tiny blaze inside the barracks, amused by the sloppy displays of joy silhouetted before them. Then, a lone, static figure caught her eye. She couldn't see his face in the darkness, but she knew it was Arin. They stared at each other across the night.

The feeling of hands on her shoulders made her jump at first, but as Roland's presence closed in behind her, she settled into his touch. Below, Arin stood up and walked off into the shadows.

"Shouldn't you be wearing a sling?" Roland asked as he gently ran his hand over her bandaged shoulder.

"I hate those things. Make me feel trapped."

"As long as you're not in pain."

It was only then that she realized. "I'm not."

He wrapped his arms around her, enclosing her in an embrace. She settled against his chest, feeling his warmth, listening to his heart. Roland's heartbeat was the first sensation she had felt after waking up in the medical lab. Back then, it was that tangible connection to the living world that had made her realize that she was still alive. Hearing it now filled her with a sense of safety, security. Its steady beat gave her strength.

"It's beautiful, isn't it?" Roland said, his voice echoing into her ear through his chest. "The sights and sounds of boundless joy gained in victory."

Lia listened with her other ear to the jubilant voices below, smiling, but soon her darker thoughts took hold. "It won't be long before they send more. Before we have to fight again."

"That I know, and we will be ready when they do. But our soldiers have proved themselves capable of facing anything that lies ahead. And they are all far stronger than they realize." He turned her face up to meet his, looking into her eyes with deep affection. "So, on this night, we have nothing to fear." His kiss helped to wash away the darkness.

The sound of Harris's voice sliced through their peace. "I need to see you, Roland."

Roland turned with a frustrated sigh. "Doesn't anyone allow for moment's celebration?"

Harris's face remained stony as he responded with a few simple words. "In the medical lab."

Roland's face followed suit. "Fine." He offered Lia a final kiss on the forehead and walked back inside without another word.

Lia was on the verge of pursuing, questioning, when Harris whispered to her, "You should have told him." He turned away and followed on Roland's heels. She was left alone on the balcony, dancing somewhere between confused and overwhelmed by dread.

It was not long before she decided to follow them.

**AS ROLAND ENTERED** the records room, Doctor Lau whirled away from the glowing screen and stared at him like a fear-struck deer. "I—I have something to attend to," he stammered. "If you would be so kind, Mister Wilson." He ushered Harris over to the control center. Once he had taken his place, Doctor Lau slipped out of the room and into the medical lab beyond, sealing the door behind him. The doctor hadn't looked at Roland with such fear since the moment he had been staring down the barrel of his gun.

*How terrible is what he has discovered?*

"It's some recalled and some recently recorded memories," Harris explained. "They jumbled together. Must be a side effect of the P.P.G. It's probably not that accurate—"

"Show me," Roland demanded. He did not want people dancing around his feelings any longer. Harris flipped a switch, and images on the glowing screen jumped to life.

It was Lianna, no more than eight years old. She dropped down from a large tree and looked inquisitively through the bars of an iron fence. The image flickered and become Lianna as Roland knew her now, looking through the crisscrossing iron of Arin's cage. Her voice, though distant, was still clear. "Roland is our commander and… my husband."

Multiple images of Lianna flashed before him, split seconds, small moments, playing out one after another—her face revealed under her helmet, her eyes filling with shock, laughing in a tavern as she tells jokes, standing in the darkness of a tunnel saying, "Someone with the means to save me." Then the screen flicked through recordings of what could only have been Arin's eyes wandering over her body, tracing across her scars as she peeled off her clothing.

Roland heard his own teeth grinding, felt his fists clenching. He breathed the tension out through his nostrils and shook out his hands, but the recordings were far from over. The next thing he saw was Lianna looking back over her shoulder as she was led out of the grand hall by Roland, deep affection and fear in her eyes, her form in such focus that Roland's was just a blur beside her. Then she was in the darkness of the tunnels again, but with her face very close, close enough for a kiss. Arin's hand was tracing over her cheek.

Roland felt his teeth snap together again, but he made no attempt to calm himself this time. Suddenly, Lianna was a teenager, wearing a gown. She was embracing, kissing, her young, idealistic eyes filled with love. Then she was running down a long-vaulted hallway, her dress trailing behind her. Arin's voice called out, "I love you." The screen went white.

Roland remained silent, his fists clenched at his side, as a whirlwind of thought and emotion overtook him. Harris eventually broke the long silence. "It was a long time ago." Instead of starting conversation, his words only stirred Roland into action. He ripped open the door and swept into the lab.

"Roland, *wait!*" Harris called out as he chased him into the lab. The sound of Harris calling out, the sight of Doctor Lau scampering into a corner, cowering behind the machinery, brought him to a standstill. Deep inside, his mind was pacing like a caged animal.

"What should I wait for?" He spun around to face Harris. "Would you suggest that I go on playing the ignorant fool? That I allow him to get away with lying to me? Let him believe he can make her lie to me? How many more times might he try? How many other lies has he already told?"

"He fought for us. He killed his own… for us. We succeeded, Roland." Harris argued. "He's one of us now."

"His loyalties are swayed by far more than politics. His intentions can*not* be trusted."

"So, what do you propose we do?" Roland had only one solution in mind. He hadn't even allowed himself to run through every available option. His first thought had been the answer. One look at Harris was all it took to convey it. "No. You can't," Harris said. Being told what he couldn't do only fueled Roland's desire to do it. "How could you possibly justify that now? What are you going to say to Lia?"

It hadn't occurred to him until then, but his first thought led him to that solution, as well. "I won't have to say anything," Roland told him "He chose to be soldier. Soldiers die in battle."

He turned to leave. Harris tried to call him back. "Roland, I really think—"

"I don't care *what* you think!" Roland shouted over his shoulder as he charged toward the door. He was done letting other people toy with what was most precious to him. He would do whatever it took to assure Lianna was always by his side and allow no one to convince him otherwise.

**ROLAND'S VOICE WAS** so loud, so full of anger, that Lia barely needed to touch her ear to the door of the medical lab to have heard every word. If it hadn't shocked her so, she would have left long before she heard his footsteps approaching, leaving her no choice but to run. She had barely started racing up the staircase before she heard the door at the end of the hall being thrown open. She had only reached the top, jumping from step to step as soundlessly as possible, before he pounded up behind her.

What could she do, let the truth flood out now in an attempt to gain some good will? It may work for her, but it was too late to bargain anything on Arin's behalf. She waited around the next corner, frozen by indecision, as Roland's footsteps closed in. She decided to let her instinct take over, to guide her through whatever she was about to face, and turned toward him. Roland tore around the corner and stopped cold. He looked at Lia with a volcanic fire in his eyes. She remained calm, betraying no emotion on the surface.

"I came to find you," she said in a placid voice.

He took two quick steps toward her. She didn't back away. She didn't even flinch. He would never hurt her. That, she was sure of. His eyes searched her face, attempting to find some crack in her facade. Rather than hide behind it, she chose to show everything to him. Lia looked at Roland with eyes full of remorse. A single tear gave him a silent apology for ever having betrayed his trust. As she brushed it away, her eyes filled with warmth and shone with unconditional love. She smiled.

He lurched forward, grabbed her, and kissed her, hard. She was stiff at first, shocked by the sudden shift in his energy, but as he held their bodies together, she let herself melt into him. He kissed her, again and again, wrapping his arms around her, breathing in her smell, taking in every essence of her being. She could feel his love, passion, possessiveness, all flooding to the surface at the same time. She knew, without a doubt, it was all being driven out by a deluge of fear. Lia grasped Roland's hand and held it tight, a reminder that she was still there with him. He finally allowed their bodies to separate but held on to her hand, and he took a step back.

"You were right," he said, without turning his eyes her direction. "They're bound to return sooner than we realize. We should already be preparing."

"I'll get the others," she offered.

"No." He finally looked up into her eyes. "You need to rest."

"Okay," she responded in a whisper.

He backed away, letting her hand slowly side out of his, then turned around and walked off without looking back.

**HARRIS KNEW IF** he waited long enough Lia would cross his path. He was certain she would have listened at the door. He was even more certain she wouldn't let Roland's plan come to fruition, no matter the risk. It didn't matter how angry Roland was now, Harris told himself, this would be better for him—for them—in the long run. He just had to hope Lia saw it the same way.

He heard her light footsteps arrive on the landing two stories above, then drop into silence as she reached the edge of the carpet. He waited as she descended, keeping her movements silent. She was impressively sneaky when she needed to be, but it was dark enough that she had to put all her concentration into stepping down each rise as lightly and swiftly as her feet would allow. She was so focused on her feet that she didn't see Harris standing in the shadows of the next landing until they were face to face. Lia drew in a breath and stepped back. She quickly opened her mouth to utter whatever excuse had just jumped into her head, but Harris spoke first.

"Go. Get him out of here." She stammered in disbelief, unable to respond. Harris pulled her into the corner where he knew their voices wouldn't rise up the stairwell. "Roland will be in the war room all night, so you'll have time. I can keep him from coming after you for a day or two but no longer. So, get him out of the city, then come back." He took an intentional pause before adding in a solemn voice, "He'll fall apart if you don't."

"I will," Lia whispered. "I promise." There was no hesitance in her voice, not the slightest doubt about Harris's last words either. She knew better than anyone how much Roland needed her. She backed away, ready to continue her descent. That's when Harris noticed the two guns in her holsters. She hadn't just prepared to run. She'd prepared to fight. But who was she preparing to fight against? The questioned raised in him a need for one last grain of assurance that they—that he—was doing the right thing. He grasped her arm, turning her back.

"Remember where your loyalties lie," he said in a firm whisper.

She only nodded in response, but the slightest raise of her chin told him she was too proud of all that she was and all that she had now to leave any of it behind. Harris relinquished Lia's arm and watched in silence as she raced down the staircase and disappeared into darkness at the bottom.

**AT THE FIRST** creak of the door opening, Arin threw his feet to the floor and wrapped his hand around his gun. Whether the intruder was an actual threat or simply another soldier attempting a juvenile hazing prank, he would make it clear that he tolerated neither. He only switched on the light after securing his aim and found himself pointing his gun at Lia. For a split second, he flashed back to their first encounter. She was dressed in battle gear, just as she was then, and starring down the barrel of his gun, yet again.

"Why are you sneaking around here in the middle of the night?" he asked as he pulled back his gun.

"You have to leave. *Now.* Get your things, and I'll get you out of here." There was genuine fear in her eyes.

"Why? Why do I have to leave?"

"Roland is going to kill you."

There were any number of reasons Arin could have imagined, but that was one he was sure had been relegated to the past. He went stony faced. "Why?"

"Because of us. Because we lied."

Despite the fear in her voice indicating she was the least likely person to have told him, Arin still let his suspicion surface. "How does he know that?"

"I don't know. All I know is that the next time you step onto the battlefield, he's going to make sure you never leave it. I overheard him say it myself."

Panic was starting to overtake Lia, but Arin found himself wanting nothing more than to puzzle together how, after all he had risked, he could suddenly become a target. "Where?" he demanded to know. "Where was he when he said it?"

"Why does that matter?"

"Because I want to know why, after fighting on his orders, after killing the very soldiers I used to command, after proving myself with their blood on my hands, why I suddenly deserve to die?" Anger had overtaken his reason and volume. She hurried to hush him before he could be overhead from the other cabins. He calmed himself and tried to switch on his strategic mind. "Tell me where."

"The medical lab."

It all became crystal clear to Arin in an instant. "The recordings. He saw it in my memories."

"That's not possible," Lia said. "The nanites were destroyed, recordings included."

"*Supposedly* destroyed by a mysterious substance created by their very inventor. Don't you think he could have taken whatever he wanted from me? Whatever he was ordered to take."

The undeniable reality of it seemed to hit Lia like punch to the jaw.

She looked as if she was trying to swallow back a tidal wave of fear that was rising inside her. She finally found her voice. "Even if that were true, why should what he saw matter so much?"

"Because in all these years, I've never stopped thinking about you." Arin tried to say the words as if they were a simple fact, but finally admitting it made his heart pound hard against his chest.

Lia took a step back, taking a moment to absorb. "We have to go."

"No."

Her frustration surfaced as she choked out the words, "Why would you stay?"

"I'm not running. Not anymore. And certainly not without knowing why. Let him tell me himself on the battlefield if that's what it takes."

Lia's fear sparked into a bonfire. "No!" she declared as loudly as she dared. "I'm not going to let that happen. I already thought you died once. I am not going to let you die this time! I am *not* letting you leave me again!"

That's when Arin knew none of this was about appeasing Roland. She would do anything to keep him safe, even if meant risking everything she had with Roland, even if it risked her own life. He stepped toward her, held her face in his hands, drawing her in close. "I won't. I promise I won't. I don't ever want to leave you again. That's why I followed you. That's why I'm fighting for you. That's why I'm here, Lia." He pulled her in even closer, bringing their foreheads together. "I will stay wherever I have to if it means I can stay with you."

They both stopped breathing. Their fears dropped away. They looked into each other's eyes and saw, for the first time, everything they had been denying, hiding, running from, and fighting against from the moment they laid eyes on each other after those seven long years. What they each had before them was the only thing truly worth fighting for. One simple kiss conveyed everything.

Another kiss, another, and another helped to push away every worry that had pressed them, every struggle they had faced, and every one they were about to. They were both who they were at that moment in time and who they had been long before. They explored each other, bodies older and different but warm and familiar. Arin traced his hands delicately over Lia's scars. She ran hers through his hair, down his back, mapping every nuance.

They made love, gliding over one another, moving both with and through each other. They breathed in the same air, eyes fixed on one another. They grasped at this timeless moment, knowing it would inevitably slip away.

**ALONE IN THE** windowless room, Roland faced no demands to play the brave and flawless commander. Without the burden of eyes and expectations, his fears had the means to take over. He had pushed them aside. He had kept them at bay. He had suppressed every itch of them on the surface with bold and decisive action. Now, in the silence, they found a voice too loud to ignore.

*What if I fail? What if she does? What if she never comes home to me again? What if everything I built falls apart? What if too many of them die? What if she is among them? What if she runs? What if I lose her forever? What if? What if?*

*What if?*

He attempted to turn his mind to planning. Thinking of the next battle, the next winning strategy, the next surprise attack, would abate some of his fears, or at least keep the better part of his mind occupied. Every time he managed to freeze his flow of doubt, it would inevitably find movement again, at first as a drip, then as a flood.

He thought about letting it take over, about racing to Lianna's side to confess to every fear he had ever had, along with every lie he had ever told her, but that would risk far more than just their marriage. Roland had an obligation to the world he had created, and it held him captive. So he ignored the questions, dismissed the doubts, suppressed the fears, and tamped it all down with an unbreakable determination to go on building all that he had envisioned and an unshakable desire to share it all with Lianna.

Though it felt as if the struggle had nearly torn him in half, the voice his fears had found grew softer and softer, shouted into an oblivion by two thoughts alone.

*This world will soon be mine.*

*She will always be mine.*

# SIXTEEN

**IN THE DRIFTING** moments between the fear that had come with night-fall and its inevitable return at sunrise, Lia remembered the fireflies.

**PAPA HAD BEEN** on another rant about her behavior. What did "proper lady" mean, anyway? Why should she have to act like a lady at all? At the age of ten, it was forever before she would even *be* a lady.

She had escaped up into the branches of the old tree. It was long dead, but she still had just enough cover from the leaves produced by its neighbors to hide from sight and keep an eye on the lawn between her and the house just in case Papa came storming out. The fireflies had started to appear, a few specks of magical light floating just above the grass, when she heard the ungraceful rustling through the bushes below her. She waited until Arin came tumbling out onto the lawn to chastise him.

"If you keep making all that noise when you come in, Papa is going to figure out there's a hole in that fence."

"Nah. He'd have to hire a gardener first," Arin said as he dusted off the leaves he'd collected on the way in.

*I shouldn't have shown that to him,* Lia thought. *He'll never leave me alone now,* though she never felt the desire to say that out loud.

"What are you doing up in that tree?" he asked, peering up at her between the branches.

"Watching the fireflies. It's the only time of year you get to see magic like this," she said as her face lit up with an inner joy.

"Magic?" Arin questioned. "It's just bugs with chemical reactions in their butts and pathetically short life spans."

Lia felt the joy immediately sucked out of her. Why did he have to ruin everything? "Don't be such a smartass!" she yelled down at him, probably a bit too loudly.

"I'm only telling the truth."

"You suck the fun out of everything. Don't you ever think that sometimes it's better not to know things?"

Arin didn't seem to have a response waiting for that one. Lia gave him an indignant nod and went back to focusing on the fireflies. She could practically hear his mind ticking away as he paced the grass below her.

After a long silence he finally said, "Well, if I didn't know so much, then I wouldn't know how to talk to them."

"Talk... to the bugs?" Now Lia was the one being a smartass, but she didn't care. Arin was definitely going to outdo her eventually.

"I thought they were more than just bugs. I thought they were magic," he said facetiously, proving himself king ass just as she predicted.

She stuck her tongue out at him and resumed her firefly watching.

"Fine. If you don't believe me, I'll show you." Arin dug around in his pockets. He pulled out a clump of odds and ends in a balled-up fist, knelt down, and dropped everything on the lawn. Lia peered down, watching a ball of string, a pocketknife, and various tiny tools spill out onto the grass. *Honestly,* she thought, *boys like such stupid things.* Arin plucked a tiny flashlight out of his pile of pocket debris. He sat against the base of the tree and watched the fireflies intensely. When the chorus of lights paused, he flashed his light, moving it up ever so slightly. A whole series of fireflies followed suit, each lighting up, one after the other, in a wave across the lawn. Arin flashed his light again, and the fireflies continue to follow.

Lia watched in amazement as their numbers increased. More and more fireflies than she thought were even in the world, let alone out on her lawn, joined the symphony of lights. Eventually, the whole lawn became a sea of tiny flickering, dancing lights. Lia leapt down from the tree, careful to pick a spot that had no magical lights hovering in it. She settled in next to Arin. He remained silent, concentrating on his task of matching his light to the rhythmic dancing of the fireflies. She could tell he wanted to gloat. That didn't matter.

He had made magic for her, even if he didn't believe in it.

**THE SOFT PINK** of sunrise was threatening to break over the horizon when Lia peered out through the crack in the door. She turned to see Arin donning his holster and believed for a moment that he would leave, after all. She laid out her plan. "We'll have to travel in the tunnels, use them for cover. There are plenty of places to hide along the way, places even Roland doesn't know about. Once we're in the next city, you can catch a transport in any direction."

"I told you. I'm not leaving." Lia prepared herself argue. "Not unless you come with me."

She was crestfallen. "I can't."

"Why?" He wasn't going to give up without a fight.

"I promised Roland I would stay here and run the guard. Keep watch over the city. If the Unis get past him, if they find Cambria, everything we fought for will be lost."

"Let someone else protect the city."

"I'm *not* leaving, Arin."

"I left with you."

"This is different. I can't just leave all of this and never look back."

It looked as if Arin was resigning himself to running again, but then he asked, "Because you love him?"

She didn't want to say it out loud, even though he already knew the answer. It came out as a whisper. "Yes."

"Are you still in love with me?"

"Yes," she said without hesitation. He already knew that answer, too.

"Then I can't leave, either." He looked at her with that same fiery determination she had seen in his eyes when he chopped down her beloved tree. This would not end until all that oppressed him was torn to the ground.

"What choice do you have?" She was trying to awaken his logical mind, to get him to weigh and balance every possibility before diving into destruction. All that did was give him an idea.

"To find out what they know. How they know it. And to uncover any other secrets they're keeping locked up in that lab." He was on his feet and headed for the door before he even finished speaking.

Lia stepped into his path. "You can't just walk out of here. Everyone will be out on the training grounds in a matter of minutes."

"Good. Then no one will be inside." He pushed past her and tore open the door.

"Arin, please!" she called out in a whisper, reaching after him. He didn't turn around. Her guns were still lying on the floor. She scooped them up, hurried to attach her holster, and began to chase after him.

As soon as Lia stepped outside, the door of the next cabin swung open. She ducked down and rolled into the shadows underneath Arin's cabin. A pair of boots kicked a cloud of dust into her face as she peered up through the break in the staircase. The talkative, weedy little soldier named Phillipe was staring, open mouthed, through the cabin door.

"Oh, you stupid bottle licker," he muttered. He leapt over the stairs to get inside. Lia watched from underneath as his shadow crossed from one end of the room to the other. He pounded back down the stairs and stood at the bottom. "You drunken horse's arse!" he said to himself. His boots turned as he glanced around, attempting to spot where Arin had disappeared to. Then he swore under his breath and took off running the opposite direction.

Lia was quick to roll out, scramble up, and race off. Roland would soon know that Arin was gone. She was certain that the next thing he would do is look for her.

**THE FEW GUARDS** Arin spotted inside the fortress were appallingly easy to sneak past. Lia will really have her work cut out for her if she expects these buffoons to protect this city, he thought. As soon as he reached the last, long hallway, he armed his gun. Arin silently crept toward the door into the lab, prepared for anyone to appear through it at any moment. Two shots at the lock made a deafening rattle around the empty corridor, followed by a loud clatter of the handle hitting the floor. Arin kicked the door open and raced inside, armed and ready.

The medical lab was eerily empty.

He took a quick survey of the tangle of machinery, prepared for someone to suddenly emerge from the shadows, but there was no sign of movement. Arin's eyes zeroed in on the locked door across the lab. With his cover already blown, he didn't hesitate to shoot open that lock as well.

He found himself in a vault-like room, which was empty except for a workstation connected to a screen that glowed with the words ENTER SUBJECT NAME. Even if Arin hadn't seen rows of stations like this in countless Unity record halls, he would still know what to do. He approached the workstation and entered TIMOTHY JAMES ARIN. An image of his own face, captured at some point while he was lying comatose on the exam table, filled the screen. Large text next to his image read SUBJECT 7,363. He scrolled down toward a block of text below and read.

Successfully injected with Formula Three. Takeover and attachment complete. 92% of formula one nanites removed intact. Memory scan in progress. Subject shows increased strength, agility, and speed. Healing ability 68% above uninjected average.

His suspicious we're confirmed, but now a new question entered his mind. What was Formula Three? His record alone would not answer this question, so Arin scrolled toward the next subject number. He searched through record after record, seeing one solider after an-

other. Phillipe's face appeared, as well the toxic-breathed soldier who
had tried to intimidate him, each with subject numbers next to their
names and notes about their increased strengths and healing abilities.

They weren't all soldiers. One record showed a young girl treated
for a broken arm. Another, an elderly man with a bad cough. Each
of those records also contained a subject number and injection date.
Arin found his fingers shaking as he entered the name LIANNA MC-
MILLAN. Lia's image filled the screen. She looked just as Arin had
remembered her every time he found himself haunted by that last encounter of theirs, but her face was deathly pale, and there were bandag-
es wrapped around her chest and shoulder. The text next to her name
read SUBJECT 0001. An extensive block of text under her image
began with—

> Injection immediately started heart and respiratory func-
> tion after failure. Full healing of extensive upper body trau-
> ma, minor residual scarring. Healing 88% above average.

*If she was the very first one,* Arin though, *then who was the next?* Arin
flicked to the next record and found Roland's image. The text next
to his name read SUBJECT 0002 VOLUNTEER. Arin's eyes raced
down the page and picked out the words—

> Subject reports on effects and submits for regular exam-
> ination. Subject volunteered for injection after the suc-
> cessful recovery of SUBJECT 0001.

Arin was suddenly driven by one desire alone, to tell Lia everything he had just discovered. He raced back into the medical lab and
searched frantically through the equipment. He pawed through draw-
ers until he discovered the boxy portable that Doctor Lau had used
to check his heart. He knew the equipment well enough to know he
could copy the records over and take them directly to her. He raced
back into the other room with the portable. In the haze of his frantic

search, he failed to see the small, hunched figured who was standing in the doorway watching his every move.

Arin plugged in the portable and set it to upload the records. He was watching the faces of each patient flick past at a dizzying pace when he heard Doctor Lau's voice over his shoulder. "Please don't tell her."

Arin spun around and aimed his gun at the doctor. He didn't flinch. He didn't move at all. He simply looked up at Arin with deeply sad eyes.

"What did you do to us?" Arin asked.

A warm smile slowly formed on the doctor's face. "I gave you the gift of life, son. Who would frown upon that?"

"But I can still be injured. She can, too. I've seen it happen. I've felt the pain."

The doctor looked up into the air as if he was puzzling out the answer to a riddle. "Hurt… yes. Suffer pain… maybe. But die just as easily…? Perhaps not." He looked straight into Arin's eyes. "But do you still value your life so little that you would care to find out? See, therein lies your strength."

Memories of everything Arin had experienced since lying on that table flashed through his mind. The pain of every injury had been intense, but he had healed much faster than he should have. He thought of Lia's gunshot wound. He had exploited her pain to save her, yet the wound was nothing but a scab the day they fought in the training room. But there was one mysterious aspect to everything he had experienced that he could not explain. "This is different. It has to be. I feel different."

Doctor Lau's smile grew broad, his energy, vastly enthusiastic. "Ah, yes! You feel!"

"So, this is, what? An improvement of your first formula?"

"*No!*" the doctor shouted, suddenly shaking with anger. "No. Nothing like the old one. No more monsters! No more cold, unfeeling machines!" He took a breath, calming himself down, then continued to explain as a teacher would to a child. "This is a natural part of you now, your body and your spirit. As the strength in you continues to grow, so will theirs. And your children, and your children's children, will be born with that strength already in their blood."

"That can't be." Arin's analytical mind buzzed with the impossibility of what he had just heard. "For that to be true, they would have to be—"

*"Alive?"* Lau proudly finished the thought for him. "Oh, there are so many definitions of the word, but they desire to stay alive so they, in turn, keep you alive. They desire to procreate, so they, in turn, procreate through us. And the fight for survival is indeed the essence of life. Wouldn't you agree?" He didn't give Arin time to answer as another wave of enthusiasm overtook him. He stepped in close, eyes wide. "They are our brothers, tied by blood with us for as long as it continues to flow."

The gravity of everything Arin had just heard was weighing on him, but all his questions were far from answered. The doctor was not hesitating to share all he knew, so Arin continued to press. "Why is Roland the only volunteer?"

The doctor stepped back as he admitted, "Not the only."

"Harris."

"Every scientist must pass his knowledge on to someone. Otherwise, how can we continue to progress, to grow?"

"Why doesn't Lia know? Why don't any of these other people know?" Arin demanded. "Why hide this substance from the very people who have it in their blood?"

"That provides the balance," the doctor explained in a professorial manner. "If she still feels, then she still fears. And as long as she still fears, then every victory is precious. Every moment an injury heals or a sickness is fought off becomes another moment to be grateful for life. Don't you see?" He stepped in even closer, a storm of zeal in his wild eyes. *"That* is perfection."

**IT WAS HIS** own fault for trusting such a scatterbrained sycophant. Harris thought Phillipe's tendency to overshare would make him the least suspicious spy possible. He assumed his obsequious nature would keep him on task. He hadn't accounted for the possibility of him drinking enough of that bottle to lay out a man three times his size. *Then again,* Harris thought, *they were meant to get away.* Perhaps his oversight was simply foresight. Why then had Arin not walked out the door while Phillipe was out colder than a fish out of water? Why had he waited until nearly sunrise? Where had Lia been this whole time? He didn't want to think about it.

Phillipe was still following his every step, spewing out excuses and apologies, when Harris spotted Roland tearing across the barracks toward them. From the combination of urgency and anger in his gait, it was clear the rumors about their most infamous recruit suddenly disappearing had reached him.

"Go," Harris ordered. Phillipe was about to stammer out another apology when he saw Roland and took off like jackrabbit.

Harris stepped into Roland's path as he approached the cabin. "I already swept it. There's nothing inside."

"His weapon?" Roland asked.

"Gone. Along with all the ammo." Roland began to pace out his rage. "We'll send out units in every direction," Harris said, trying to dilute the anger he saw building up with every step. "He won't get far."

"Send them into the underground," Roland instructed. "He knows the way in and therefore the way out."

"Of course."

Harris had faltered just enough for Roland to know he had intentionally not mentioned the underground. Roland turned toward him, barring down on him. "Where is she?"

Even in the face of rage, Harris knew he could answer honestly. "I don't know."

"You're lying," Roland said through his teeth.

"I don't know, Roland!" Harris snapped back. Doing what little he could to keep an innocent man from dying, to hold Roland and his marriage together, was not something he would let Roland chastise him for, even if he'd had to keep a few secrets in the process. "She's not the one you asked me to watch."

Roland didn't bother to direct any more of his anger toward Harris. He absorbed every grain of it as he whirled around and took off across the barracks. Harris knew that whatever Roland would do next would be decided by whomever was the next person to step into his path.

# SEVENTEEN

**ARIN SEARCHED FOR** Lia with as much strategy as his desperate mind could muster and as much speed as his feet would allow. He stuck to the shadows, peering around each corner before silently racing down the next hall. He would not let himself get caught. He would not become a prisoner again. He would not leave until he told Lia everything. So, his search went on, winding up and up, as he climbed farther and farther into the heart of the fortress.

**LIA RACED UP** the steps two at a time. She didn't have to go through the broken door of the medical lab to know that Arin had already left. Doctor Lau's crazed eyes staring at her from the other end of the hall told her everything. She was sure that Roland already knew Arin was missing. She held out hope that she might encounter him in the hallways, that she might be able to assuage his anger before he pursued him. She would do whatever it took to keep Roland from coming after him. If Arin was the first person she found, she would do whatever it took to get him as far away as possible. So, Lia ran from floor to floor in a frantic dash to prevent their paths from colliding.

**ROLAND'S BODY HUMMED** with overflowing rage. He would use it as fuel in his pursuit of Arin, but first he would find Lianna. He didn't have to think about where he was going. Every grain of his being pulled him toward the stronghold. Anyone else would have headed into the underground, would have assumed they were on the run with a few hours lead to their advantage, but something in Roland's core told him Lianna was still inside. Whatever else—whomever else—he might encounter in his search for her, he would deal with as need be. He raced in the direction which he was led by instinct, pulled by fate, knowing it would inevitably lead him to her.

**ARIN FOUND HIMSELF** heading toward the doors that led into the cloistered courtyard he'd insisted on exploring when Lia attempted to lead him past. He cracked them open and peered into courtyard on the other side. Morning light had yet to fill in the shadows, but it appeared empty. He opened the doors, just wide enough to slip through, and sealed them silently behind him.

*"Arin!"* Lia's voice called, somewhere between a whisper and a desperate plea. She raced through the opposite doors into the courtyard. They met in an impassioned embrace at the center. "Why are you so stubborn?" Her voice wavered. She threw angry fists against his chest. "Why do you insist on proving yourself when your life is at stake?"

He held tight to her, keeping her close. "You have to leave with me, Lia. He's been lying to you. This place—this whole army—it's not what you think." Arin put the portable into her hands. The records began to scroll past, endless names and faces flicking across the screen.

"What is this?" she asked, confusion in her eyes.

"Everyone the doctor has injected with some type of new nanites, ones we wouldn't notice, ones that don't make us feel any different. All of us, injected without our knowledge."

"No. That can't be true." Even as she said the words, he could hear her doubt seeping in with them.

"They've been using this formula for years. It's in thousands of people. It's inside both of us." Arin showed Lia her own record.

She stared at it, her eyes racing frantically through the text. She suddenly went pale. The portable slid from her hands and clattered to the stone below. With unfocused eyes, she asked, "Why was I the first?"

"It was the only way to save your life," Roland's voice answered from the shadows of the arcade. Arin and Lia spun around. Roland emerged into the spill of morning light, gun in hand but held down by his side. He walked toward them, slow, calm, methodical. "By the time I got you to the lab, you had already lost too much blood. You were moments from death. The formula was the only chance you had left." His voice was as steady as his movement. He had prepared for this moment, but Arin was not going to make any part of this confession easy for him.

"No, you needed to see what was going to happen," Arin protested. "You needed someone to test it on." He turned back to Lia. "You were just an experiment."

Roland's arm snapped up. He pointed his gun straight into Arin's face. "Don't you *dare* define what she means to me!"

His voice boomed around the courtyard as he charged, gun first, at Arin. Arin had just begun to raise his own pistol, preparing to take a bullet and deliver one at the same time, when the appearance of Lia's gun at Roland's temple stopped him in his tracks.

Arin used the moment to fix his own on Roland.

With the quick *click* of a safety, the cold barrel of Lia's other sidearm pointed into Arin's temple.

They locked into a three-way standoff, Lia's guns pointed at both of them.

Arin peered down the barrel to Lia's face, trying to read her intentions. Surely she wouldn't shoot him, but she would never shoot Roland either, yet there they were. The truth Arin had been so desperate to share with her had unlocked both her fear and her fight. Now it was just a matter of which would take over. She glanced back and forth between them with a look in her eyes that made it clear she had taken charge.

Neither of them dared to move.

**HOW HAD IT** happened? How had she come to be standing there with guns pointed at the two people she trusted the most, loved the most? Lia summoned up the voice to ask, "Why didn't you tell me?"

Roland spoke without taking his eyes, or his aim, off of Arin. "What would make you fear pain and suffering if you knew you would always recover? What would keep you from taking advantage of those weaker than you, simply because you could?" Then he turned his eyes toward Lia as he asked, "What would make you any better than them?"

"But I *am* one of them. You've turned me into a *machine!*"

"How can you say that feeling what you feel this very moment? Your eyes are tearing, your hands are shaking. I know you're afraid. You're every bit as human as you have ever been."

Roland was right. Her petrified pulse was hammering away in her throat. Her shoulder was screaming in pain as she forced her torn-up muscles to hold her gun steady. The jumbled mix of shock and betrayal churned inside of her already fear-struck body. What was she so afraid of that she suddenly didn't understand who or what she was anymore or that she may have never known who, or what, Roland was?

"How could you do this to us?" she asked, her voice fading.

"Not just us." Arin said. "And not just the other soldiers. Every person that has ever seen the doctor."

"We helped them. We *saved* them." Roland's eyes were pleading.

"Without telling them how. Just so you could make people believe that the weak can be strong, that the sick can heal, that the dead can come back to life." Arin's voice was finding more strength, his gun arm straightening.

Roland's was softening, his focus fixed only on Lia. "People need to believe, to *feel.* It's their humanity that saves them, not the technology in their blood."

"You've intentionally hidden the truth so they'll think they're stronger because of *you!*" Arin shouted. His certainty was growing. Lia's was crumbling.

Roland was not done making his case. He preached to Lia and Lia alone. "All I want is to make this world human again, allow people to fear, to celebrate, to suffer, to love." There was so much sincerity in his being. Lia could not tear her eyes away from his.

Arin let out an aggravated breath. "You're turning people into something they don't even understand, something they didn't ask to be, for what? Vengeance?"

Roland's eyes flicked over to Arin, a flash of anger sparked to life. He took a step toward him. Arin stepped back. Lia pushed through the pain in her shoulder and the tremors in her hands to firm up her aim, keeping them locked in a triangle of steel. They froze for a moment of tense indecision. Who would be the first to move, to speak?

Roland suddenly took a step back and allowed his gun hand to drop. Arin lowered his gun but kept his aim fixed on Roland. Lia let herself relax just enough to provide a hint a relief to her shoulder but would not pull back either pistol. She didn't trust anyone at that moment.

Roland looked up toward the square of sky above them as if it held the answers, then turned toward Lia with eyes that were nothing but warm and genuine. "This wasn't created to rule us, but to better all of our lives equally. To make all of us stronger without taking away our fears or desires. Our children will be born into a better world, Lianna."

"Our *children?*" The notion mystified her. Roland was speaking of it as if it were the only future he had ever envisioned.

"When I started to build an army, it was all for the sake of taking the world back from the Unity, at any cost. Everything has changed now. All I want is to build a better world and share it with you."

There was an uncharacteristic humility in Roland's posture and a depth of fear in his voice. Lia felt as if she were melting on the spot, her guns suddenly too heavy to hold straight. She hadn't even realized she had lowered her arms until she felt Arin take hold of one.

He stepped in close. "He's been lying to you for all these years. What's going to stop him now?"

**WHETHER IT WAS** the sound of his words or the sight of his hand grasping his wife's arm Roland felt a sudden explosion of rage launch itself at Arin.

"The first words you ever spoke to me were a lie! Everything you pretended to be since you arrived is a lie!" He charged at Arin. Let him shoot if he dares. Let them end it right there. As long as Roland didn't have to hear any more of his acidic accusations.

"Stop! Stop it!" Lianna screamed.

Something thumped into Roland's chest. It was Lianna's hand. The white knuckled grip around her guns had turned into shields. She was holding them both back, using herself as a barrier neither of them dared to break. She let the echoes of her scream die down and took in a deep, trembling breath before she spoke again.

"Please, tell me the truth, Roland," she pleaded softly.

He had been. All he could do now was keep telling her over and over until she believed him… if she ever would. He stifled the hurt of her disbelief and answered. "I am. All I want is a future, a family. All I want is you."

Lianna didn't have any time to take in his words before Arin was forcing his upon her again. "It's another lie. All you want is victory. All you want is a kingdom."

That same volcanic explosion of rage took over Roland's body.

He heard himself say, "And I'm not going to let you take it."

He felt his arm snap up.

He felt his finger pull back on the trigger.

He heard the *bang* of the gun, followed by Lianna's scream of genuine terror.

Roland didn't step back into his own body until Arin's hit the ground.

"No. No!" Lianna dropped to her knees. A pool of blood began to form around Arin's head. "You can't be hurt. You can't be killed. You have to heal! You have to *live!*" She shook his body. "You have to come back.... You can't leave me like this again.... Please... don't leave." Her voice faded. His unblinking eyes stared up to the sky. The pool of blood grew larger. She broke down into manic tears.

Roland had long feared the moment Lianna would learn the truth of her miraculous recovery. The dreaded sense that is was inevitable had awoken him in the night more times than he could count. These circumstances were something he never could have envisioned. Her sobs over the body of a man who had tried to turn her against him, her devastation, was debilitating. He desired nothing more than take her into his arms and pacify her anger, alleviate her sadness, and placate his own guilt. He took a step toward her. She instantly snapped up and pointed a gun into his face. Her flow of tears immediately stopped as she stared at him over the barrel.

Roland tossed his gun to one side and fixed his eyes on Lianna's. "Tell me I was wrong to save your life." He found renewed strength when he heard his own voice and dared to take another step toward her. "Tell me I was wrong to instill in you all the strength that you have now, that I'm wrong for wanting to give that to the entire world." He took another step and put his forehead in line with the barrel of her gun. "Because if you can... then shoot."

Her finger traced around the trigger. She began to squeeze. He held his breath, looked fearlessly into her eyes, and prepared for his own death.

She froze. Her hands began to shake. Her tears welled up again. She dropped the gun down by her side. Roland, once again, felt the overwhelming urge to take Lianna into his arms, but she swiftly backed away, tears streaming down her face. She turned and ran, disappearing back into the depths of the stronghold.

Roland's fears all screamed out at once, their voices cacophonous. He dropped his head into his hands, attempting to suffocate the thoughts before they took hold. Then, he heard a footstep behind him.

Roland whipped around to see Harris walking slowly into the courtyard, his eyes scanning the scene laid out before him. He stared contemplatively down at Arin's body, at the pool of blood around his head, then looked up at Roland. He had nothing to say. The circumstances that led here were obvious and the result now lying in the middle of the courtyard. Roland straightened up, breezed right past Harris, and left without uttering a word.

# BEGIN AGAIN

# EIGHTEEN

**EIGHT MONTHS LATER,** the emergence of the New Resistance Army had begun to change the face of the world. Three attempts by the Unity to march into the unknown territories beyond the badlands had met with three miserable failures and a staggering number of casualties. Even more surprising was the subsequent loss of every border city the Unity had secured over the last few months. Resistance territory was expanding.

Those who saw the battles spoke of them as if they were clashes between mythical forces of enumerable strength. Stories about the Resistor's ability to materialize as if from nowhere, to tear down their virtually indestructible foe, to fight on through any injury, had found their way from village to village, spreading like wildfire around the fringes of the world. The Resistor's reputation for walking away from each battlefield with little to no loss was often attributed to the skills of their formidable leader.

In the center of the hidden sanctuary in the middle of the desert, Jakes and the barmaid danced, arm and arm, with their fellow villagers. At the peak of the mountain a funnel of black smoke rose from a pile of burning bodies, but inside the valley, music and celebration abounded.

In the heart of Caldera City, Johnson and Rita drunkenly stumbled out of the tiny eatery in the lane-way. They raced toward the city square so they could cheer on a group of Masons as they lowered the large Unity flag and tore it to shreds.

Roland was to give a speech to his loyal soldiers and citizens of

Cambria, the capitol of the new Resistance world. In the overcrowded barracks, soldier's jockeyed for the best position to look up toward the balcony on which he was about to appear. Crowds packed the streets, rippling with excitement. People watched from the farms at the border just to get a distant glimpse of their fearless leader.

All of Cambria roared with applause when Roland finally emerged, with Lia by his side. She may have been standing on that balcony, but her mind was far from the jubilation below. She turned her eyes down to examine her own pregnant form. She put her hands on her body and gently caressed the life forming inside of it. A small smile appeared on her face as she felt her unborn child stir.

Far below, a dark figure stood alone, unmoved by the celebration. No one in the streets would have recognized him. No one would have known the role he played in the sudden start of this unexpected war. No one would have suspected the secrets he carried about the beloved leaders they were cheering for. No one could have known what he and Lia had once meant to each other, so Arin allowed the sunlight to caress his face as he looked up toward the balcony.

He waited and waited for Lia to turn her eyes away from her future child, for her to sense that his gaze was fixed on her, for her to pick out his face among the thousand others. Lia's eyes never looked out toward the crowd.

*It doesn't matter,* Arin told himself, *we'll find each other again.*

He dropped his head, pulled the hood of his jacket up around his face, and disappeared into the shadows.

**WRITER AND FILMMAKER** Margaret M. MacDonald is passionate about telling stories which transport people into other worlds and make this one a little more extraordinary. Her visual writing style, shaped by her background as a designer, conveys a tangible sense of place, inviting readers into the story world. Born and raised in the United States and currently living in Australia, Margaret likes to bring a mix of both cultures into her work. She has written a library of screenplays and novels in a mix of genres, has directed several short films, and has been lucky enough to win a few awards along the way. She enjoys embracing a creative challenge and wants, more than anything else, to tell a story audiences will love.

Milton Keynes UK
Ingram Content Group UK Ltd.
UKHW011134220424
441551UK00006B/533